The Urbana Free Library

To renew: call 217-367-4057
or go to "urbanafreelibrary.org"
and select "Renew/Request Items"

YOUR FATHER
SENDS HIS LOVE

STUART EVERS

YOUR FATHER
SENDS HIS LOVE

STORIES

W. W. Norton & Company
Independent Publishers Since 1923
New York • London

For information about permission to reproduce selections from this
book, write to Permissions, W. W. Norton & Company, Inc.,
500 Fifth Avenue, New York, NY 10110

For information about special discounts for bulk purchases, please
contact W. W. Norton Special Sales at specialsales@wwnorton.com
or 800-233-4830

Manufacturing by RR Donnelley Westford
Production manager: Beth Steidle

Library of Congress Cataloging-in-Publication Data

Evers, Stuart.
[Short stories. Selections]
Your father sends his love / Stuart Evers.
— First American edition.
pages ; cm
ISBN 978-0-393-28516-1 (hardcover)
I. Title.
PR6105.V48A6 2016
823'.92—dc23

2015029784

W. W. Norton & Company, Inc.,
500 Fifth Avenue, New York, N.Y. 10110
www.wwnorton.com

W. W. Norton & Company Ltd., Castle House,
75/76 Wells Street, London W1T 3QT

1 2 3 4 5 6 7 8 9 0

L.I.B., C.V.E.

CONTENTS

LAKELANDS

The men were called to stop, to down tools, to come and listen. He heard and saw it from the crest of the hill, looking down onto the building site: the foreman's fingers-in-mouth whistle, his waving of hands, the gradual hush of machinery. He watched his father, the last to stop and wipe hands; the last to join the gathering men in the gathering silence. This is how he remembers him: sweated clothes, a clumsy shuffle, apologetically tardy. A look on his face, worn often, of overwhelming concern. No sound of blade on brick, no cement churn, no excavation of earth. Just the quiet framing him.

The son stood and with the stolen telephone took a photograph. He shot photograph after photograph; the shutter-sound following each rapid tap. His father was to the right of the foreman, still wiping his hands. The son focused on the foreman: his fatty face and stained teeth, a too-small hardhat on Irish curls. He talked slowly. He shook his head. Nothing he could do. The son moved the viewfinder to the workers, shot them in their questions and anger, then back to his father, still wiping his hands on the rag.

The foreman finished his speech and the men disbanded: unhappy, angry. The son shot them fetching their belongings from the Portakabins, some no more than youths, lighting cigarettes, kicking the scrub, kicking the weeds. His father stayed where he was, looking up to the sky, down to the dirt. The son pinched the screen until his father's face was in his hands. He took one last photograph and switched to video. Again his father looked up to the sky, down to the dirt. The son was still taping as his father made for the Portakabins. Men smoked and heaved holdalls over shoulders, called to one another, organized which pub, pointed their fingers at the foreman.

When his father emerged he was clean and dressed in casual clothes; hair wet, a third darker, covering the grey. The foreman back-clapped him, the only one still there, saw him out and locked down the site.

The boy took more photographs. The left-behind machines and materials. Plastic flapping in a soft breeze. The suggestion of houses. The ruins and scatter. He thought of the *Marie Celeste*. Her sailors gusted into the atmosphere, harvested by someone, something. The son took one last photograph, the wire-mesh fence up close to the phone's lens, then went back to his bike and backpack, lay down and scrolled through the photographs. The son watched the site emptying then filling, emptying then filling, until it was time to head home.

*

Remember this. Remember when. Always remember. In the period immediately before leaving a town, his father would briefly turn to the future, all his talk of how much better it would be somewhere else. But this was always short-lived. Within a week of arrival he would wind backwards. Remember when. Remember how small. Remember the smell. Remember the neighbour. Remember what I told you. His oilcloth face, age and weather blessed, smiling sometimes, always with that word on his lips.

But since arriving in town the father had only looked forward. Even his long body and tightly compacted waist affected a progressive lean. A week after starting at the new site, he'd walked his son across town, through the park and a council estate to a large area of fenced-in scrubland. They'd walked the perimeter, calves cramping at the gradient. When they reached the crest of the hill, his father stopped.

'Birdseye view,' he said.

Wasteland surrounded a man-made lake, its water furred with algae.

'But don't look at it as it is now,' he said, 'imagine what it will be like!'

From the back pocket of his jeans he unfolded an artist's impression of Lakelands. He handed it to his son and they looked over it, orienteering for the future.

In the artist's impression, the lake had been dredged and reconditioned, a narrow shoreline running beside it, stock-image couples taking an afternoon's walk along the track. Stock-image families picnicked on the kidney-shaped grasslands, while stock-image dogs played ball with stock-image children. To the east of the lake, a stock-image man left the boathouse, sailboard under his arm, heading to join those already catching the breeze. Stock-image lapwings and stock-image grebes were added to cloudless, unraining skies; and in driveways stock-image residents unpacked groceries from their stock-image cars. Mostly though there were houses. Hundreds of them; brown-roofed and toy-like, all looking out over the lake.

'Imagine it,' his father said. 'The two of us living here, by the water's edge. Just imagine!'

'I'm trying,' the son said.

'Wouldn't it be great?'

'Amazing,' the son said.

'There's a deal,' the father said. 'The company are offering an amazing deal. Discounts. No money down. We could live here, if you wanted. We really could.'

The son looked at his father, the way he gripped the artist's impression.

'I'd love that,' he said.

'Really?'

'Yes. Really.'

'I wanted to check. I wanted to be sure,' he said. 'Because you said you liked the school. But I just wanted to be sure. Honestly, these are the best houses I've ever seen. En-suite bathroom. Good-sized gardens. Look at them. Imagine living in one of those. Look at that view!'

He grabbed the boy into a clinch. The boy could hear his father's heart. His father laughed. He laughed all the way home, even when a summer squall quickly drenched them. They stopped off at a pub and drip-dried in the canopied beer garden.

'This'll be our local,' he said. 'We'll come here and you can have your first pint. Legal pint, that is. Then we'll walk home. Maybe we could start fishing. Night fishing. A camping stove. A tent to sleep in.'

'That sounds great,' he said to his father. 'Just great.'

When they got home, his father tacked the artist's impression to the kitchen wall. It overlooked them as they sat at the table, each imagining the future as they ate breakfasts and dinners.

The morning after the foreman had closed the site, his

father stared at the stock images, eating cereal without concentration; drops of milk on the grey of his stubble.

'I lost track of time,' his father said, still looking at the wall. 'I'm so sorry.'

'It's okay.'

'It's not. I should have called.'

He looked at the boy, saw his own young face. Shorter hair on the boy than him, though; run through with clippers.

His father got up from the table and placed his bowl in the sink.

'What did you get up to yesterday?' he said.

'Up to the rec,' his son said. 'We played football. It was like eighteen-a-side at one point. Some kid chipped his tooth and there was a bit of a fight. Jordan and me, we went down the town too. Sat in the park, watched the world go by.'

'The girls go by?'

The boy said nothing. A bow of the head.

'Today?' his father asked.

'Jordan and me might go watch a film. There's a whole load of us going.'

'That a hint?' His father smiled, took a note from his pocket and handed it over.

'Thank you,' the boy said.

'You're welcome,' his father said. 'I can't remember

the last time I went to the pictures. I'd like to go some time. Perhaps we can go together one night?'

'Won't you be late?' the boy said. 'It's twenty to.'

'Yeah,' his father said. 'I should make a move.' He stood.

'See you later,' his father said. 'Love you.'

Kiss. Kiss. Same as wherever. Whenever. Kiss. Kiss, on the cheek, on the crown of his head. And then gone.

*

The boy looked down on the development. Around the foundations and shells of houses, heaved dirt settled in heaps. He took photographs. A video, five minutes or so. Hands held as still as he could, but with a tremble to the film. He watched it back while sitting cross-legged, sandwiches close to hand.

He played the video four times. Midway through, a bird landed on the fencepost and looked around. Should have been a vulture, but instead a starling. A couple more joined it soon after, then left; their chattering just audible.

He watched them fly away and was about to press play again when he noticed a woman standing beside him: grey-blonde hair, baggy jeans and a zipped-up fleece, looking over Lakelands. There was no lead, no dog snuffing the weeds and grass.

'So what happened?' she said. She sounded like a

teacher, one of the many; soft voice, worn with caring and its lack.

'I don't know,' he said. 'Yesterday, they just stopped.'

'I heard them take the equipment last night,' she said. 'Hell of a noise.'

She made a quick puffing noise with her mouth. He went back to the screen, pressed play again.

'I've seen you here before,' she said. 'I live up there' – she thumbed back to the thin line of houses airbrushed from the artist's impression – 'and every morning I see you. Every afternoon. With your phone and your sandwiches.'

He pressed stop on the video and took a photograph of the woman.

'I thought you might know what had gone on,' she said.

'I don't know any more than you,' he said.

'Oh, I doubt that,' she said. 'I very much doubt that.'

She kicked at something in the grass with her unbranded sports shoes.

'I'm sorry to have bothered you,' she said.

'Sorry,' he said. 'If I knew, I'd say.'

The woman looked like someone who had once worn too much make-up and now wore none at all. The kind of woman his father was always letting down; never quite living up to his first few months of promise.

'Goodbye,' she said and began to walk home. He heard her stop, then walk back to him. She stood just behind, out of his range of vision.

'Would you mind if I asked you a question?' she said.

'What's that?' he said.

'Why do you come here?' she said. 'I mean, young lad like you. Sitting here all day long. All day on your own?'

He took another photograph of her; zoomed in close on her face. The photograph was pixelated, blurred as she moved her head. He looked at the screen. She was there in his hand.

'To take photographs,' he said. 'That's all.'

She looked down with eyes that sagged and a mouth unsure where it should settle. She nodded.

'Can I see?' she said.

*

Years later, safe and snug in Luca's arms, he lies in the quiet of the room, the two of them coiled in sheets. It is after midnight and the plates and pans are stacked in the kitchen sink, left for morning. They have eaten osso buco, made by Luca, Elliot as sous chef, in honour of Luca's parents, flown in to visit. The flat is too small so the parents took a taxi to their hotel, kisses and fussing as they left. Luca dozes, too much wine with his dinner, unnecessary grappa. The wardrobe door is ajar; their clothes hang side by side, still a surprise. On the floor are their jeans, soft legs on hard wood.

'Can you not sleep?' Luca says.

'I like your parents,' Elliot says. 'Your father especially. I can see where you get it from.'

Like his father, Luca is a storyteller in several languages, a barroom flirt and centre of attention. His arms are hawserish, his body gym-built, protein-shook. But soft inside, so soft.

'They liked you too,' Luca says. 'That's what all the Italian was about. You.'

'Me?'

'Of course, what else?'

Luca moves his arm over Elliot's chest.

'Sleep. It's late.'

'My father was more the silent type,' Elliot says. 'He would have struggled to get a word in edgeways tonight.'

Luca looks up from his pillow, red-gilled and sour-smelling. Hairless legs and chest uncovered, his buzz cut and cheekbones move towards Elliot.

'My father can be a bit much,' Luca says. 'He wasn't always like he is now, you know. It took him time. After I told him I mean.'

Elliot can feel the measure in Luca's words, the care not to seem leading. He is grateful for this, though he feels the question beneath the calm. Others have been more explicit.

'You have that faraway look,' Luca says. 'Guilty schoolboy look. Hand out; smack me now, sir, look.'

Elliot puts his hand around his wrist, so thin now, better now, thin; hair too now, lots of hair on his body, worries once that there wasn't enough, or too much, and now no longer a worry; his penis no longer a cause for concern too, all those nights of anguish and just a cock now, and he looks at Luca waiting. The bedroom is close and silent.

What he wants to say is simple. He wants to say, 'Luca, I am not a good man.' But he does not. Luca will only disagree, count the ways he is good. Elliot would like to shock Luca, but cannot.

Luca's arm is on his chest, his eyes pale grey and attentive. He waits.

'My father was a good man,' Elliot says. 'He was a good, good man.'

*

Three days later the woman stood beside him again, still dogless, wearing what looked like the same clothes.

'Still here, then.'

'Yes,' Elliot said. 'I have more photographs, would you like to see?'

He scrolled through the images, back, back and handed her the phone. She was quick, did not take her time, and with this Elliot was disappointed. She passed back the phone.

'I liked the other ones more,' she said. 'You have an eye for people.'

'I wondered if you'd notice anything,' he said. 'It's only something small. You know, like one of those spot-the-difference puzzles. Look again?'

He put the phone back in her hand and stood behind her as she swiped. She finished the set and worked backwards. She pushed out her tongue in concentration, the way his father did while working a screwdriver.

'What am I looking for?' she said.

'You'll either see it or you won't. It took me a few times before I noticed it. I don't know how many times.'

On the fourth run-through, she paused and swiped back, forward, back.

'I think I see something,' she said. 'Is it this?'

She zoomed in on one of the unfinished houses. Elliot nodded.

'Well spotted,' he said.

'When you see it, it's obvious,' she said, swiping forward until the house was clearly three feet higher than it had been in the earlier image.

'You're quite the detective,' she said.

'My name's Elliot,' he said.

'I'm Clare,' she said.

'It's nice to meet you, Clare,' he said. 'I'm glad you came back. I wanted to say thank you.'

The woman puffed out her cheeks.

'Thank me for what?'

'Last time you saw my photographs, you said I had a good eye. I should have said thank you.'

'Well, you're welcome,' she said and laughed; a chirp, used for batting away the odd compliment. 'I think you're better with people. Those ones of the three builders were really something.'

Elliot looked up at the woman. The conversations they might have. She turned to the development, to Lakelands, and shook her head.

'Well that didn't take long,' she said, nodding towards the site. Elliot turned to see five kids running between the bricks and foundations.

'There'll be an accident,' she said. 'You mark my words.'

Elliot picked up the phone and began taking photographs.

'Don't you join them,' she said. 'Don't you get yourself hurt.'

'I won't,' he said.

'See you around,' she said.

*

He heard the front door open then shut, and from his bedroom window looked down on his father, holdall on his back, hands inside his jacket, toe-cap boots dangled around his neck. The father stoop, the father shuffle. Elliot dressed and put on his trainers at the front door, decided against the bike. The streets were cool, sodium-lit, lamps behind curtains and blinds, no cars on the roads at this hour, a motorbike whine somewhere in the distance. They had lived in towns where there had been sirens at night, but this was not one of them. Remember the police cars? Remember the ambulances, all day and all night? Never heard anything like it, not even when your mum and me lived in Newcastle those years.

Through the park he half ran, avoiding dog shit, a spray of vomit, a smashed bottle of something. The playground was in the process of being rebuilt, made safe; the bowls club was locked tight, graffiti ghosting beneath its recent paint job.

On the council estate he kept his head down and turned the familiar streets. He thought of the woman on the hill, her voice's knowing timbre as she passed back the phone. She knew. It was all there in the photographs. All those close-regarded arms and legs, strained neck muscles, strip-shirted boys with tattoos and smooth-hardened stomachs. (Many years later, when asked by yet another straight man how he'd finally come out, he'd just said it was the moment he showed a strange woman some of his photography.)

Elliot breached the crest and looked down onto Lakelands. His father was working a plot close to the lake. He had a storm lamp set up, a board of mortar in his left hand and a trowel in the other. Elliot zoomed in on his father's working face, its wild vacancy. The soft light, the scrape of the mortar, the laying of brick. He took hours. Sweated hours. The bricks stacking, flush and red. His father must have laid hundreds before sitting down against the wall and taking a can of beer from his holdall.

The fence was easier than he'd thought to scale; but the drop was long and hitting the ground felt like it would shatter his feet and shins. He lay at the foot of the fence. The light from the storm lamp was uninterrupted by shadows. Elliot walked slowly towards it. His father was damp faced and pale. He did not look surprised as Elliot sat beside him.

'Dad?'

'I was just thinking,' his father said. 'You remember

how your mother used to hate me drinking out of cans? Used to say, "You're not on the building site now, love, get a bloody glass."'

He laughed.

'You remember that?'

'Yes,' Elliot said.

'Of course you do,' he said. 'You remember everything, you.'

He drank from the can.

'Did you follow me?' he asked.

'Yes,' Elliot said. 'I heard the door go, saw you leave. I was worried.'

'You knew?'

'I guessed. You've not been right these last couple of days.'

'Remember when your mum failed her driving test?'

'She cried for days.'

'Yes, she did. Soppy cow, your mother.'

He hadn't mentioned the driving test in years. Driving even. His father drank his beer and shook his head.

'It's just a job, but still. This time. You know? I thought it had to be this time. Got to be this time. But.'

He laughed and shook his head.

'Just for once,' he said, 'I wanted to do something for us, you know? Get something that was ours. The two of us—'

'Dad,' Elliot said. 'I need to tell you something.'

His father put his can in the dirt and sat up. He was straight backed. A schoolboy, hands out.

'What's that, son?'

'It's important. I need to tell you something.'

He laughed and grabbed the boy by the arm. He hugged the boy close to him, beer and sweat and the father smell.

'It's going to be okay, son. I promise you that. I love you. I love you to the ends of the earth, no matter what. You know that, don't you?'

'Of course.'

'So tell me. Tell me your news.'

And he did. And his father held him close. And his father said, 'To the ends of the earth, son. To the ends of the earth.'

*

Luca runs his fingers through Elliot's hair. Elliot is allowed to stop here; Luca has given him silent permission. They are enough, these words. They slay the fears. A good man.

'He was old-fashioned, my dad. A tough guy and quiet, yes, but a good man. He believed in goodness. A code of behaviour. It was the only thing he demanded of anyone. When he said "you're a good lad" it was the highest compliment he could pay. It was what he valued above all else.'

Elliot half laughs.

'He loved my mother. He wanted only for her to be happy. He was the same with me after she died.'

Elliot shakes his head. 'A man like that is a danger to himself.'

To the ends of the earth.

'I used to love watching him work,' Elliot says. 'I would create jobs around the house for him; pull off door handles, smash locks, damage windowpanes just to see him get out his tools. Such concentration! It was hypnotizing.'

His favourite of all the photographs: his father carrying a hod of bricks, his expression utterly absented in effort.

'The summer I was fifteen, the last summer we spent together, I used to sneak up to this building site and watch him as he worked. It was the happiest I'd known him. I took photographs of him. They captured him, I think. That was the summer I told him.'

The beer and the sweat and his smell.

'I think he was relieved more than anything else. No more pretence, no more questions about girls and who was attractive and who wasn't. I knew he knew. I wasn't even worried when I told him. He was proud of me, he said. I remember him saying that as if it was the first time he'd ever said that word. Proud.'

Luca kisses him. Elliot says nothing and waits. Kiss. Kiss. Same as wherever. Whenever. Kiss. Kiss, on the cheek, on the crown of his head.

Elliot remembers the hospital. The sheets and machines. The time they took off the bandages, the itch of the plaster casts.

'And then he lost his job. Or had already lost his job, I don't remember. He didn't tell me. He just wandered the streets trying to get something else. He seemed fine, though.'

Elliot shifts down in the bed, doubles the pillow over.

'It was fine, it was all going to be fine and then, I was walking by the site, the one he'd been working on. It was supposed to be all locked up but these kids were there. They were just messing around. But then they saw me. And that was that.'

Luca touches Elliot's cheek.

'How bad?'

'Pretty bad. It was a small town. What do you expect?'

Luca shudders. Mirror reflex.

'They jumped me. Six of them, five, I forget. I was in the hospital for a couple of weeks. Dad sat by my bedside. Wouldn't leave. He told me stories about my mother. About the three of us. Stories I hadn't heard before. And

I watched his anger. I watched it grow. I watched him swell with it. Lying there, I watched a good man just . . . drain away.'

The blows, the release, and then the coming, rushing pain. The woman who liked his photographs somehow materializing beside him, a siren coming. Hold on, her saying, hold on. In the pain, in the sound, the paramedics helping him, green uniforms, and the thought of his father. His father later, at his bedside, putting headphones over his ears, playing songs he could just about hear, muffled beats, and the smell of vending-machine coffee and unwashed skin and nothing for it but to listen.

'When I was up to it,' Elliot says, 'the police came and they asked me what had happened. I told them I'd been jumped by these kids. That they'd called me faggot, queer, cocksucker as they punched me, kicked me, pissed on me. They wrote it all down in their notebooks and Dad was shaking. He said nothing. The police asked me for more information. Who the kids were. If I knew them. I said I didn't. I'd seen them around, but I didn't know. They left without believing me.'

His father standing as the police left, looking at his son.

'You tell me,' him saying. 'Tell me now.'

'I told them all I know.'

'I don't believe you.'

'Dad, please. I don't know them.'

And his father shaking his head. Him crying. Him putting his hand to Elliot's face.

'I'm sorry,' him saying. 'I'm so sorry.'

'How he found out, I don't know,' Elliot says. 'It was a small town. No secrets, I guess. A week later the nurse came in with a policeman. They showed me a photograph. Asked if I recognized the kid. I said I didn't. They didn't believe me. They told me that the boy in the photograph had been attacked. His father too. My dad had taken a hammer to the both of them. The kid had managed to run away, but Dad broke the kid's father's arms instead. It took three men to get him off the guy. They said he was lucky to be alive.'

Luca's arm on his chest still, heavy there.

'I only saw him once more after the trial. I went to visit and I don't remember what he looked like, or what he was wearing or anything. But I remember he sat across from me and said, "Remember the houses." He said, "Remember the houses down by the lake?"

'"Yes," I said. "They were good houses."

'"I would have liked to have gone night fishing with you there," he said.

'I'd brought him this map thing we had of the housing development he'd been working on. I gave it to him and said he could have it for his cell wall.

'"You keep it," he said. "It's yours." And he smiled then. He asked how I was feeling and he didn't listen. He was just remembering. That's all. Just remembering.'

Elliot stops talking. Luca does not say anything. There are shadows from the blinds on the wall, Luca's arm is heavy on his chest. A good man.

*

For three days he photographed the boys. He shot them throwing bricks into the lake, jumping down into foundations, swinging on pieces of scaffold. One he half-recognized from school. They would arrive mid-morning and stay until bored. They pulled wheelies on their bikes, dared each other to do ever more dangerous things. His father's house grew each day, a whole wall now constructed. He wanted to show the woman his new photographs, but she never came.

On the fourth day the kids arrived later. They skimmed stones on the lake, set some small fires, watched them burn out. The one he half-recognized organized the other boys into factions and they played some kind of war game in the scrub. He saw the boy point to his father's house. To their house. He saw him say something he couldn't catch. All five boys started for the house, sprinting. There was a whooping, like the call of birds.

The boys began to climb over the shell of the house.

One of them had a spray can and tagged the underside of a window frame; another dangled his legs over the wall, hollering into the sky. The one he recognized was picking still-damp mortar from the brickwork. Elliot ran down the bank and climbed through the hole the kids had made in the fence. He waved his arms as though shooing pigeons.

'Get off that,' he shouted. 'Get off that right now.'

The boys turned to the noise and saw his quick approach. They looked amused. They jumped down from the house and walked towards him. The one he now recognized stopped. Elliot did the same. The one in the middle pointed at Elliot.

'Hey,' the kid said. 'I know you. I fucking know you. You stole my fucking phone.'

And the boys ran for Elliot. They ran for him and he could not move. In the breaking summer light there was nowhere for him to hide.

FREQUENCIES

Diwali lights in windows, on doors, on fences. The boy and him looking out over the yards and gardens. The bang-bloom of nearby fireworks; the bigger, brighter lights of organized displays. The boy chewing on his rubber giraffe; its hoof, its neck. Dean's phone to his ear and her voice quietly muffled. He's okay? Yes, he's okay. And he's had his bath? Yes, he's had his bath. And you heated the towel? Yes, I heated the towel. You're not by the window, are you? No, I'm not. How are you doing, love? I miss you. You miss me? He misses you too. I miss him so much. I know. I love you. I love you too. A still in the sky, the last firework spent.

The boy's room was cramped: a cot, a chest of drawers, a toy box, a small armchair. Dean sat down and tested the milk. A drop on the wrist, performed as rote, as seen on television. It slid off his wrist, fell onto his jogging trousers. Milk drips ran down the fabric. He didn't like them washed often, so Rachel took them when he wasn't looking. The jogging trousers disappearing and reappearing, long and damp on the airer, so big beside the boy's small tops and bottoms.

The boy took the bottle, eight months and a bottle now before bed. As a child, Dean had imagined the sound of fireworks to be a war coming; its bombs and gunfire. He looked down at the boy. At Jack. He watched the suck and rush of his neck. Jack's eyes were open. His eyes open to confirm this was not his mother holding the bottle. Dark skin and dark eyes and the constant mechanical suck. Dean stroked the boy's tight curls, brushed the tops of his ears. There was an old desk lamp bent at the middle, the bulb directed down at the foot of the cot. A late, straggling firework popped. The boy kept sucking. Dean stroked the hair on his son's head.

Dean and Rachel had married at twenty; their lack of other sexual experiences a shock to others. As their friends' relationships became soured and twisted, hoarse from shouting and bitter from drink, Dean and Rachel's home was a constant: a calm place to hide, a sofa on which to sleep, a place of caring and safety. When Dean and Rachel later managed to secure a mortgage on a two-up, two-down, their more infrequent guests swapped the sofa for their own room and bed.

By their early thirties, Dean and Rachel's relationship had become underscored by a quiet yet growing sense of trauma. The friends who'd crashed their sofa got married and Dean and Rachel went to their weddings. The friends who'd crashed their sofa had children, and Dean and Rachel went to their naming parties and christenings. The friends who'd crashed their sofa asked them to be godparents and Dean and Rachel politely declined. The IVF was an expensive joke.

There were three treatments, no results, and no money for a fourth. They stopped trying. They saw a cousin of Rachel's, sixteen years old; heavily, laughably pregnant. They sat in parks with friends surrounded by babies and toddlers and children. They were ashamed at their thoughts, their imagined interventions. They tried talking about it, they tried ignoring it; they went on as if normal. They got drunk one night and scored drugs in nostalgia for their teenage years. They fucked for an hour and in the morning Jack was mistaken for bad guts and comedown.

The boy was in Dean's arms, sucking still. The boy's eyes were closing, his mother not coming. His mother on her way to Harrogate for a conference. Her and the boss, Doug Hopkins, and the sales manager, Bill Sewell, in the same hotel. For the weekend, she would staff the small stand in the conference hall while the two men went out canvassing, trying to sell their services. They worked in glass: conservatories, replacement sash windows, skylights. She'd started as the receptionist, been promoted to secretary, then to PA to Doug Hopkins himself. Doug Hopkins wouldn't know what to do without her. Doug Hopkins relied on her. Doug Hopkins needed her. A hundred pounds in a brown envelope at Christmas. A box of chocolates on her birthday. Monday after the conference off in lieu of the lost weekend.

Dean looked down at his son. Dean stroked his son's hair. When people asked about his son, Dean hardly dared say anything. He was scared of jinxing the normal conception, the normal pregnancy, the natural birth; scared of jinxing it retrospectively. Dean stroked his son's hair. Quietly he hummed a song; a tune that soothed the boy almost to sleep.

He held Jack to his chest. He rocked from hip to hip, the way he and Rachel both now did, the way their friends rocked from hip to hip. The boy was breathing against his neck. Tiny breaths. Tiny breath against his jaw. The boy snored sometimes. A snuffle that could not be synthesized. A sound unique to him, though Dean knew there was nothing unique about it: it was just the sound of an eight-month-old boy with a head cold.

Dean put Jack down on the mattress. The sleep-suit was warm and downy, but Dean covered him with a blanket anyway, one Rachel's mother had knitted. It was well-made: cable knit, baby-boy blue, needled with love. He kissed the boy on a curl, turned on the baby monitor and walked to the door. He looked back and held his breath, heard the boy breathe and closed the door.

From the fridge he got a can of beer and from a drawer took out a pizza delivery menu. It had been devised for people who were bored with pizza. There was something called a Chunky Monkey which had banana on it; another had a base ringed with a hotdog sausage. He would order what he always did – ham and mushroom, as large as they came – but he looked up and down the columns anyway. So many options.

As he phoned through the order, he thought he heard something from the monitor. He put his palm over the handset. He heard the boy's breath, the dead air, the white noise of the quiet house.

'I'm sorry,' Dean said to the pizza man. 'What was that?'

'Be about half an hour to forty-five minutes,' the pizza man replied.

'Thanks,' Dean said.

He took his beer into the vacuumed lounge; Rachel had done it before she'd left. She'd tidied away the play-mat and stowed the toys in a cardboard box, shunting it behind the armchair. Three bars on the fire and its sidelights gave a soft, adult kind of glow. He sat down on the red sofa they hadn't yet paid for and turned on the television. There was a film he'd recorded, something she would not watch. He thought of Rachel arriving at the hotel, the way she would be dressed, the picture of Jack in her purse, on her phone. He pressed play and watched a man kill another man using a plastic shopping bag. The victim sucked in the last of the air; his eyes went slightly, then completely. Dean drank his beer. The title music began and he turned down the volume, glancing at the baby monitor; its brow of lights, its plastic-grille speaker. He put it to his ear, the boy's breath. He put it down and went back to his film.

Rachel called as the killer slashed a man's eye with a razorblade. Dean pressed pause. He saw the aftermath on the screen as he said hello. He turned off the screen. His beer was almost finished.

'Hey, love,' she said. 'I've just got in.'

'You made good time.'

'Yes, it was fine in the end. How is he?'

'Fine. Asleep.'

'Did he get off okay?'

'Yes, no problem at all.'

'You ordered your pizza yet?' she said. There was bathwater running in the background.

'What's that?' he said.

'Have you ordered your pizza yet, cloth-ears?'

'What makes you think I've ordered pizza?' he said. He was smiling a little; she was a fine and regular tease.

'You always order pizza when I'm away. Always.'

'How do you know? How do you *know* I always order pizza?'

'Because I love you and I know you better than any-one else in the world and because you always leave the box unbroken in the bin.'

He laughed and walked into the kitchen for another beer.

'I might have ordered a pizza,' he said. 'But you can't be certain.'

'I'm naked,' she said, not listening. 'Naked's different when you're in a hotel, isn't it? Feels different, anyway.'

He opened his can of beer and watched the suds poke through the hole like wool. 'That was a lovely hotel we went to, that last time.'

'We should do that again,' she said.

'Yes,' he said. 'Yes we should.'

The quality of the call changed; the slight echo of the bathroom, the sound of her turning off the taps. A bath-room bigger than their bathroom no doubt; a bath bigger than their bath.

'I used to look forward to you going away,' he said. 'Years ago, I mean. Nothing too exciting. A pizza, some beer. Footie on the Saturday. Something on the video. Sounds sad, doesn't it?'

'Don't you look forward to it now?'

'No,' he said. 'No, I don't look forward to it. I miss you, you see. He misses you too, I can tell.'

'Oh, don't say that,' she said.

He saw her sitting on the lip of the bath, cool plastic on her warm behind.

'I used to look forward to it too,' she said. 'Staying in a hotel. Fried breakfast every morning. All of that. I still do a bit.'

Dean heard something on the baby monitor. Something brushing something else, something moving. He put his palm over the handset, the white noise of the quiet house.

'Everything okay?' she asked.

'Everything's fine, love,' he said. 'I thought I heard the doorbell, that's all.'

*

Dean woke as the killer shot a man through the kneecap; his screams childlike and loud, exactly like Jack's. He looked over to the baby monitor, but the bulbs were dark and he only heard the dead air. The killer shot the man through the other kneecap. Dean wanted to know how much research they'd done, whether they'd watched someone put a bullet in a man's leg for real, or whether this was guesswork and imagination. As he turned his head he was briefly looking neither at the screen nor at the baby monitor. At that moment he clearly heard a male voice say: 'Interesting.'

The lights remained out on the monitor; he heard the boy's breath. He had definitely heard a man's voice, an older voice, one that sounded familiar. Even had the killer on the video been the kind to make a remark after a kill, it could not have been his voice. Dean pursed his lips. He picked up the baby monitor again. He put it down and had a sip of beer. He waited in the near silence, eyes on the monitor. After a few minutes Dean rewound the film at 64x speed, back through what he had missed. He saw five frames: a grenade, a knife, two guns, a pair of breasts, a man with his head in his hands. He pressed play and the speed was out for a moment, the voices not quite synching. He heard the same voice clearly say: 'I have no interest.'

Dean pressed pause and in his haste hit the button twice; the picture stuttering, starting, finally resting. A gun to the head of an air stewardess. He looked at the baby monitor, its unlit bulbs. He heard a voice say: 'I have no interest in talking about my childhood.' And after that an elderly male laugh. He heard the boy's breath, the dead air, the white noise of the quiet house.

He did nothing. There was nothing to do. He pressed play on the film. He drank the rest of his beer and was reminded of the chill opening of a church door. Following his father into the nave, the hot light blasting the stained glass, the birds, crucifixes and men. Watching his father walk, crane-necked, to the altar, then cross the aisle to where two small candles burned. His father dropped coins into a metal box and took a candle. He held a flame to the taper, watched it catch, and fixed it beside the others. In Jamaica, his father was dying, was dead, was on his way to hospital, was eating his dinner before the heart attack. Dean had never seen his father enter a church before; Dean had never seen him light a candle. As they left, Dean asked his father why.

'Sometimes you just know something and you just don't know how,' he said.

Dean supposed it was all to do with frequencies. A radio interfering with the signal; a pirate station did the same when, as a kid, he used to listen to BRMB late at night. The man's voice was interference, nothing more. He looked at the plastic speaker, the snub aerial, the red, green and orange LEDs. He heard Jack move and an elderly man's cough. The voice said: 'People talk about their childhood and it's so mundane. I don't remember much about it, if I'm honest. I can't even tell you what my father's voice sounded like. And that's the truth.'

The background hiss suggested the voice had been pre-recorded and was now being broadcast. He heard the boy's breath again. The broadcast had stopped. He picked up the monitor and put it back to his ear.

'I'm not even sure I would recognize my mother and father. They were such dull people. Such short and dull people. So very short and so very dull.'

And then again his son's breath: in out, in out. You could count those breaths for comfort. And then a cough, whether on the recording or from Jack it was not clear. On the baby monitor, the red light flickered, and down in the bottom right of the speaker he heard a recorded laugh, low and embarrassed. A short laugh without humour.

'There is a saying,' the recording said, 'that the children of lovers are orphans. It suggests something mythic, something epic about the nature of romantic love. It casts romance as murderer; as assassin. They were not epic, my parents. They were dull. Short and dull. They loved each other, my parents. There is no denying that. But it was without heroism. Together they wanted to be good parents. More than anything that's what they wanted. Cruel, isn't it, desire?'

Dean turned off the baby monitor. He left it there, adrift, powered-down on the sofa, and went upstairs. He opened the door to Jack's room and sat on the armchair. He looked at his son. The boy's breathing was soft and regular. Dean moved the chair so he could look out of the window, out over the yards and gardens, and at the boy sleeping. He texted Rachel – *I love you, goodnight* – and listened to his son breathe. In out, in out.

*

Twelve minutes past seven and the boy had his hands on the bars of the cot, prisoner crying in foggy morning light. Dean picked up the boy, held him to his chest and the boy made clicks and dada noises with his mouth. The nappy was full; sweet and rotten, like old apples. More clicks and more dada. He looked down at the boy. At Jack. The boy would not hold his gaze; he went rigid as Dean wiped him down. He wriggled and tried to turn over.

His scream was siren-loud and sharp. The second and third the same. Three of them, short burst, long shriek, short burst.

'Jackie,' he said. 'Come on, quiet now.'

The boy still would not look at him. Short burst, long shriek, short burst. Dean smiled and gurned and made noises. One long shriek now. Still the boy would not look at him. *I'm not even sure I would recognize my mother and father.*

Dressed after a long and bitter fight over socks and a jumper, Jack sat in his high chair. The television was tuned to a children's channel. They tried not to have it on, but they couldn't argue with the fact it soothed him. Dean heated porridge in the microwave, warmed milk on the stove.

'Everything okay?' Rachel said. He had the phone crooked in his neck as he sliced a banana.

Her hotel room would already be untidy, messy without him around.

'Yes,' he said. 'Did you sleep well?'

'Not really,' she said. 'He's eaten his breakfast?'

'I'm just heating it up now.'

'Check it's not too hot. Be sure to stir it up well.'

'I know,' he said.

'Are you sure everything's all right?' she asked.

'I didn't sleep well either,' he said.

'Oh, love. To be expected, though, don't you think?'

'I'm sure you're right.'

'Put him down for his nap at nine.'

'I know.'

'What time are you heading over to Andy's?'

'Just after he's had his nap.'

'Don't let poor Lena look after all the kids while you watch the football.'

'I won't,' he said.

'I need to go,' she said. 'I love you so, so much.'

Long, long shriek.

'I love you too,' he said.

Jack took the milk and ate the porridge and didn't once look at his father, his eyes only for the television. He was sick after eating, his clothes covered in it. Dean looked at his watch. Under two hours before nap time.

'Your mummy will be home tomorrow,' Dean said after two hours of screams, soft play, watching the boy crawl. Jack was chewing on his rubber giraffe, its hoof, its neck. Dean pulled down the blind and put the boy in his sleep suit. 'She'll be back and it'll all be good. Sleep time, now, yes?'

The boy went down without complaint. Dean watched Jack breathe as he ran through what he needed to do before the boy woke again. Rachel had made a list of what needed doing and most of it was focused within this two-hour period. Lunch and dinner preparation, unloading the washing machine and reloading it. He looked at Jack and at the baby monitor. Its plastic speaker, the snub aerial.

'Oh for fuck's sake,' he said and closed the door behind him. He turned on the monitor when he got to the foot of the stairs. He put the monitor on the kitchen counter and began the washing up. He unloaded the washing machine, hung out the clothes on the airer. He put in a new load and set it to 40 degrees, added a detergent tablet and turned the dial.

'I never hated my parents,' the recording said. 'Hate is too emotive a word. Pity is the word I would use. Pity, yes. I pitied them.'

Interference. Nothing more. Something to do with frequencies.

'I pitied my parents,' the recording said. 'Pitied them even before I knew what the word meant. I know I said I remember nothing of them, but just saying that has made me recall something. They would take me to Sunday school. I had forgotten this, but it is true: Sunday school. And I was sitting reading a magazine. In the magazine was a cartoon of a boy saying to another boy, "Your drawing's good," but he was thinking, "But not as good as mine." And next to this was another cartoon with the same scene but the boy saying, "Aren't our paintings good?" and thinking, "Together our paintings are really great," and underneath it said: WHO WOULD GOD BE HAPPIEST WITH? I didn't know the answer. I could not understand what God would want me to do. Because the first panel, the one I knew was the supposed "wrong" answer, was truthfully what I would have done. It was like God had looked into my soul and found me wanting. He had found me wanting, and found me pitying my own parents: "Your lives are good, but they're not as good as mine."'

Dean slid down, down onto the lino of the kitchen floor. He sat there, knees up, his hands on his thighs, listening to the voice.

The first time they had taken the boy out they'd dressed him in layer upon layer of wool and cotton. Rachel wore her best maternity clothes and tried not to worry about bleeding. They took him to a nearby town and pushed him around a large church, around grave-stones. Inside the stained glass radiated light. The candles were electric, two men and a woman were praying. It wasn't like the place in which his father had lit a taper. On the way out, Dean put a pound in the donation tray. As they walked past the graves and back to the car, he wished he'd given more.

'I would have loved to have been a tearaway, a rebel, a fighter, a truant,' the recording said. 'But their faces, their demeanours prevented it. They looked at me as though I held the secret to the universe. As I amassed language, I used it as a weapon against them. It was the only way to shame them. Bad behaviour and tantrums were met with cloying faces, with the same looks of blessing. One cannot rebel against people or structures that are satisfied only by one's existence. The only rebellion would be one's own death, and even then, even in infancy, I was very much taken with the possibilities of life. A school-mate died. I remember that now. I do not recall her name.

She drowned in a lake. Ten years old. She was young for her age, boyish. I once saw hers and she once saw mine. I told my parents about her death and realized my error. I felt the already narrow room close in, their attention and vigilance subtle yet wholly obvious. I felt the ache of their love for me and it was exhausting and brutal.'

Rachel went through eleven hours of labour in the hospital and, as she pushed, Dean could not believe how anyone could survive the violence; but then the child came and screamed and it didn't matter. In his arms; the tears and the tears. The we're-going-to-have-such-fun-you-and-mes. The fingernails.

'I cannot remember a single thing my father said to me,' the recording said: 'his voice is permanently muted. My mother's the same. I'm always amazed that the dull-witted and ugly fall in love, aren't you? There are no photographs of them in my possession. I have none of their belongings. I sold the house without returning and was given a sum for its contents. Heartless is such a harsh word to use, don't you think? The point is to be honest in this life. I rate honesty as the highest of all the human virtues. Honesty will set us free. The honesty to be the person you truly are. I left home as soon as I could and I never looked back. I made my indifference quite plain, yet still they loved me, loved me right until the end. And that is all there is to say about my parents. I will say no more on them. There are far more interesting things to talk about. Far more interesting things.'

Dean got up and began chopping a carrot, then an onion. The onion was strong, the house silent. He put the ingredients for the chicken stew in a pan and turned up the heat. He then got a hammer and smashed the baby monitor into small shards of plastic and speaker. He gathered up the bits and put them in the rubbish bin, then took out the rubbish.

When he heard Jack screaming he ran up the stairs, just as a father should; just like that, exactly as he should. He opened Jack's bedroom door and the boy had his hands on the bars of the cot.

'Hello, Jackie. Are you awake now, boy?'

Jack looked at his father, eyes straight ahead.

'Dull,' the boy said. Clearly, distinctly.

'Dull,' he said again. Dean could see a new tooth.

Dean picked up his son and put him to his chest. Tears were in his eyes. He held his beautiful son and wished Rachel was there to share in the moment.

THESE ARE THE DAYS

He warmed the teapot and through the kitchen window watched her spit on the backyard flags. Dark out, the light from inside illuminating her. She had her back to him, her hands on her knees. He saw horizontal lines of filth and silt and sand lashed up her calves. Thin lines, pale skin. He saw her breath, pit-horse clouds from mouth and nose as her back heaved. She spat again, her saliva a silver coin on the stone. He watched her turn towards the house. Framed between parted yellow curtains, she saw him in the window. Dark out, light inside. She jumped, jolted like the ground was wired live. She clasped her hands to her chest and mutely laughed. He watched her shake her head as she approached the house.

She opened the door and shut it on the dark. He was still by the window, still holding the warmed pot. She brought in the smells of outside: of sea and sand and wind and spray; of cooled sweat and unbrushed teeth. He watched her take off her running shoes. Pink and yellow and green. Mud-raked, difficult to unlace, small when placed on the backdoor mat.

'Good run?' he said.

'Yes,' she said. 'I took your advice. From the jetty to Peacehaven, then back.'

She was tall. Taller than him, over six foot, surely. He gave her a bottle of mineral water from the fridge. She took it as though there was always mineral water in the fridge. She drank – one, two, three – neck bobbing; a thin channel of water running from the corner of her mouth. He watched her shake out her ponytail, strands of dark hair coiled like coastlines on her forehead. Holding herself against one of the chairs, she stretched out her right leg. The sheer fabric of her shorts reached down to her knees. The shorts were skin-tight, good for support, he supposed; coloured flashes down their sides. The athletes on the television wore them. They provided minimal wind resistance. A pocket at the base of the back for keys or a wallet perhaps. Tight muscles of her calves, tight muscles of her thighs. From the jetty to Peacehaven, then back.

'Everything okay?' he asked.

'Just need to stretch, Grandpa, that's all. Be fine in a minute.'

He spooned out tea leaves. Three teaspoons: one per person, one for the pot. He filled it with boiling water and set it on the table. Somewhere there was a tea cosy. He couldn't remember the last time he'd seen it, let alone used it.

He watched Anna unzip her running jacket. Black with yellow and green trim, reflective surfaces, good for safety. The T-shirt underneath was yoked with sweat, the fabric thin and engineered; designed to 'wick moisture away from the body' – salesman's words that sounded impressive when he'd bought it for her last birthday.

She hung the jacket on the back of a chair and looked across the kitchen to the stove. The frying pan was already on the unlit hob, beside it a butter dish, a carton of eggs, fatty bacon in greaseproof paper.

'Don't wait for me,' she said, nodding to the food. 'You eat your breakfast.'

'Oh no,' he said. 'We'll eat together, you and me. You take your time. Have a bath, a shower, whatever you want. There are towels in the airing cupboard, nice and warm. We'll have breakfast when you're ready. There's no rush.'

Her socks were tiny. He watched her quick-disappearing footprints on the laminate. Bobby socks, at the hop. Earphones trailed from a device strapped to her upper right arm. On her wrist, a rubber-coated watch continued to time her run. From the jetty to Peacehaven, then back.

'I didn't know if you'd be awake,' she said. 'I know you said, but . . .'

'Us old bastards get up with the larks,' he said. 'I blame the sea.'

She laughed at 'bastard'.

'I do,' he said, 'it's like an alarm clock for the retired and useless. The whole street's up before sunrise. Probably the whole town. In the summer at four, five in the morning the coastal path's full. If you see any of us approach, run away, that's my advice. Run away from us old bastards and keep on running!'

Anna giggled, put her hands on her hips; stretched to the left then to the right. Her joints cracked as she rolled her shoulders. He watched her kick out her legs. The muscles in her arms were defined and tight. Mens Sauna and so on. She walked past him, the half footprints on the laminate following her.

'You're the funniest old bastard I've ever met,' she said.

'You're a lousy liar,' he said. 'But I'll take any superlative as a compliment.'

*

Soon after her fifteenth birthday he began to write her letters. There had been a family gathering for Anna at his son's house, and Ben had made one of his quarterly excursions from the seafront to the city. In the late-summer sunshine he briefly caught up with his son and daughter-in-law, then retired to a corner of the garden to drink red wine with a widower and a divorcee of his own age. Sitting at the rattan table, top buttons undone on their waistbands, they looked like close, old friends.

Whenever the conversation took a tedious turn, Ben would stare past his companions to Anna across the lawn. She was curled up on a picnic blanket with her three best friends, fingers worrying at the shorn grass. As he passed them on the way to the bathroom, he overheard their conversation.

'She makes me write thank-you cards. *By hand*. Can you believe that?'

'Serious? Not even email?'

'No. Must be handwritten. Takes for ever.'

'By hand? Serious?'

'What's the fucking point in sending a letter?' Anna said.

There was a stationery shop at Victoria station and before boarding the train he picked up some writing paper – cheap, flimsy stuff, but writing paper nonetheless – and an ink cartridge for the fountain pen he never used.

The following morning, sitting at the kitchen table, he wrote:

Dear Anna

It was lovely to see you at your birthday celebrations yesterday. While I was there, I overheard you ask why people write and send letters. I hope the following answers your question.

We write letters for the way they make the recipient feel: for the elation caused by their discovery on the doormat; for the thrill in recognising the sender's handwriting; for the delightful promise of the tearing of the envelope (though using a letter-knife is even more wonderful!); for the physical and emotional exchange that only a handwritten letter can provide.

I am not against technology, far from it (you should see me go on the Internet!); but if you do not feel any of these emotions upon receipt of this letter, I will happily receive an emailed thank-you note in future. I am – for once – confident, however, that you will understand why we still send letters, and perhaps even correspond with me in this most venerable of ways.

I shall watch my doormat with eager eyes.

Love always,
       Grandpa B

Anna's response arrived a week later, written on a page torn from an A4 notepad.

Dear Grandpa B

Thanks for the letter. And thank you very much for the book and the H&M vouchers. I can't remember ever having got a handwritten letter before, and I loved it. I am busy with exams at the moment, but when they are over I will write and tell you how they went.

Love from
    Anna

Over the next six years he wrote whenever the urge took him. He was pleased with the way his script curled and the neatness of his hand. He often prefaced his reminiscences, or things that had occurred to him, with, 'Forgive me if I have written this before . . .' He wrote, 'It is a curse of old age to one day assume you have said everything, and the next assume the opposite. Each is as tedious to the recipient as the other.' This he could remember writing, sitting in the pub on the other side of the Seven Sisters, his trousers roasting by a fake open fire.

Anna's replies were erratic, though she never forgot a

thank-you note for a Christmas or birthday gift. There was a period of six months when she sent him a letter every two weeks, but mostly they were spread-out, badly written, poorly punctuated, scrawled on good-stock paper (his gift to her each birthday). He kept her letters in an unmarked suspension file. He had no idea how many letters he had written. Hundreds, he assumed. When he read through her letters, he wondered whether she kept his, and what the sum of those letters would say about him. Perhaps she had thrown them away, destroyed them as though never written or read. Still he wrote the letters. Still he licked the envelopes and affixed the stamps and walked to the end of the road to post them. Still he listened for the postman's trolley on the pitted asphalt.

*

Anna sat down at the kitchen table. She smelled of things the house had never before encountered. Shea butter, cocoa beans, jasmine, spearmint. The sharpness of it cut the musty air. His aunt's house had smelled of trousers worn too long, of undried clothes, and he hoped his house did not smell that way.

'Here you are,' Ben said. The radio was on. He poured tea into her cup. Blue-green, with a white interior, the kind they used to have in cafes. Matching teapot. She poured in milk from the jug. They had always done this. From the jetty to Peacehaven, then back. Him at the window, tea-pot in hand. Preparations for breakfast and then her taking her place at the table, hair in a towel turban, a sloppy T-shirt and sweatpants. Here you are. Pour the tea.

As he beat the eggs and warmed the grill for the bacon, she checked her messages. Her nails on the screen, clicks and clips like a telegraph operator. He watched her, her eyes intent on the glow. He remembered a line from a song – *these are the days of miracle and wonder.* Anna sighed, muttered something he didn't catch over the sound of his beating eggs. His ex-wife used to do the same while reading the morning paper. He would ask what was wrong, but she could never quite manage to communicate her displeasure. The thing is. What he's saying is. What they don't understand is.

He remembered the singer's name as he placed the bacon on the grill pan. *Would you not say, Anna,* he wrote in bed that night, the writing pad propped on his knees, *that all days are full of miracle and wonder?*

He sliced the toast diagonally and arranged it with the eggs and bacon on both plates. She typed until the very last moment. He put the plate in front of her. The smell of her; the smell of salt and fat, the piping lines of steam from the eggs.

'This looks grand,' Anna said. Ben nodded and smiled. Grand. Yes. She had said it twice since her arrival. Things were grand. Things were not grand. He watched her construct a forkful of breakfast. She grinned and nodded as she chewed, pointed with her knife towards the plate in approval. He ground pepper over his eggs. The woman on the radio said 'tyranny'.

'I was thinking,' Anna said, 'I might stay a day longer. If that's all right.'

He pretended to be distracted by the radio. He heard the word 'atrocity'.

'Of course,' he said. 'Please, stay as long as you like.'

'Thanks, Grandpa,' she said.

He would have said something then, but there was a soft beep and Anna looked from him to her device. She crossed her cutlery and for the rest of the meal tapped and typed without apology. He watched her idly noose a strand of hair around her finger, the way the finger went red, then white and then slowly back to pink as she released it. *These are the days.*

In bed that night he wrote: *The breakfast I cooked was hearty; too hearty for me. I usually eat thin toast. With all that running though, you need the energy. Maybe I should begin to run. Perhaps then I would sleep better. Am I too old to run? Would I look ridiculous in pink and green and yellow training shoes? When you come again, let's run together on the seafront . . .*

He picked up her plate. The bacon's fat had been

delicately removed; the bread was untouched. He looked down at her and saw her father's bow mouth and wide eyes; her mother's haughty cheekbones and tiny ears. Hairline from her paternal grandmother, his ex-wife; chin-line from her maternal grandfather. Nothing, save for the crease of her brow, to call her own.

'That was delicious,' Anna said. 'Thank you.'

'I'm glad,' he said. The man on the radio said 'uncertainty'; Anna sat with her elbows on the table, the heels of her hands together.

'You haven't asked,' she said.

'Asked what?' he said.

'Why I'm here.'

'Do you want me to?' he said.

'No,' she said eventually. 'No I don't.'

She got up from the table.

'Thank you,' she said. She picked up her phone and made a call as she walked through the sitting room.

*

He had been decanting a batch of soup from the stock pan into a third plastic container. Thick-sliced ham, specially cut off the bone at the supermarket. Home-made stock. Potato and cream and salt. He used to make it when the boy was ill; telling him it would make him fit and strong again. Also for his now ex-wife, for his mother when she was latterly fading, and for himself, for himself mainly, over the last twenty years or so. He listened to the radio and checked the clock. Dark outside, light in. A glass of wine. Two.

The telephone rang. In the letter to Anna he wrote the following evening, he described himself answering it like *a washer woman, drying her hands on a rag as she made her way from kitchen to hallway.*

'Grandpa B?' Anna said.

'Oh, hello, Anna,' he said, like this happened always: her phoning, him picking up, him drying his hands on a dishrag. He switched the receiver from one hand to the other.

'How are you?' he said.

'I'm not too far away from you,' she said. 'Brighton. Can I stop by?'

Instinctively he looked at his watch. He knew what time it was. He knew almost precisely. But still he looked. A little after eight.

'Of course,' he said.

'Would it be okay if I stayed?' she said. 'I'm tired and I don't want to go home tonight.'

'I'll make up the spare room.'

An hour later, her car – small and snub, snooker-baize green – pulled up outside. Ben was at the front-room window quite by chance. He watched its headlamps die.

The driver-side door opened and his slender, tall grand-daughter got out. He watched her stretch. Long arms high in the air. He watched her remove her handbag from the passenger seat, slam the door shut and from the boot remove a wheeled suitcase. He watched her drag it up the short pathway.

'Hi,' she said. At the door, in the lamplight.

'Come in,' he said.

After he'd shown her the bathroom and to her bed-room – sheets newly clean, carpet vacuumed – they sat at the kitchen table. He had uncorked a bottle of wine he'd bought on a day trip to France and spooned out bowls of soup for them both.

That night in bed, the writing pad balanced on his knees, he wrote: *Perhaps I drank my wine too quickly, but I don't recall all of what we talked about. Where you might go for a run, yes. The shops in the town. The traffic on the motorway. I remember what I didn't say. I didn't tell you that I'd thought about calling your father, but didn't. I didn't ask you why you'd come to see me when you'd never stayed with me before. I didn't ask you any-thing I didn't know the answer to. I sat at the table with my soup and I did not wish to add to the weight. I just did not want you to leave. I didn't ask because I didn't want to know; I didn't ask because I feared you'd leave.*

*

Outside, behind the fence, the heads and hats of walkers; the sea beyond them, a tanker just before the horizon's tuck. He was scrubbing the grill pan. The sink was black and tan from the grill, the pork fat curdling the water. He pulled the plug and turned on the hot tap.

'This is a lovely house,' Anna said. He turned from the sink to her. She was dressed in jeans and jacket, boots already on.

'You think so?'

'Yeah. Reminds me of your old house. The one in Northampton. Like that, but smaller.'

'I'm surprised you remember it,' he said. 'You must have been very young.'

The family house in Northampton. Bought on the cheap using money they didn't have. How many years there? Almost thirty. Should not have stayed there as long as that. After Val left, should have sold up and moved on. But no. Unable to move, unable to think. A house with a child and a wife, and then just him. His job, his house and walks in the park. Call it mourning. Val always said he was the sentimental sort.

He'd had no intention of moving, and had only done so because an estate agent pushed a flyer through the door. He retired then. Took it early. For quiet by the sea. For a different view. For beach walks and hikes across cliffs and afternoon drinks in comfortable, open-fired taverns. For his grandchild to visit on weekends and on holidays.

'Whenever Dad asked where I wanted to go or what I wanted to do, I always said I wanted to go to Grandpa's house. To go to that big park behind your house. I thought it was your garden at first,' Anna said.

'You were five,' Ben said. 'I remember you coming then.'

He had lived in Seaford for almost fifteen years now and had never considered the new house's similarity to the old. Anna was right: it had the same layout, the same proportions. What had been his son's room, upstairs at the back of the house, was now the spare room, Anna's room. The small room where his wife would banish him for snoring was now a place for his junk and his computer. The master bedroom, his room, their room, where his son would impose himself in those early years, a little boy between man and wife. The five cookery books on the shelf by the cooker had been on a similar shelf in the previous house. The potato peeler on the washboard, the spoons and bowls had survived from that time; the kitchen table too.

'There were the most amazing swings.'

Little Anna in the park that afternoon, running and chasing the rain in her wellington boots. Red wellington boots, a hand-knitted coat, a cold, cold nose. His daughter-in-law picking her up, taking her back to the house as the two men talked.

'What do you want me to say,' his son said. 'What did you expect?'

His son was no longer his son, but an unknown man with side-whiskers and a paunch.

'You can't blame her for moving on,' he said, and his look said where the blame lay. The wind caught Ben's anger. The things he said, the volume at which he said them! And his son just standing there, watching him. Almost confused. On the edge of laughter.

'You're angry because you didn't see it coming. That's all,' his son said. 'She says she's happy. She looks happy. Happiest I've ever seen her. So you leave her alone. I want you to promise me to leave her be.'

Ben took a step towards him and the boy's stance changed: on point, the jaw set and clenched. Ben walked past him and back to the house. The boy shouted something the wind and trees caught and Ben did not turn around. He needed to hear it from her, from Val, not from his son, with his unsmiling mouth. From the house, he telephoned her. He called her and she did not answer. From the bedroom he heard them getting ready to leave. They did not say goodbye.

Anna standing now in his living room. Grandchildren grow so much more quickly than your own.

'And how is your father?' Ben asked.

'Fine,' she said. 'Dad's fine. Mum too.'

'That's good,' he said.

'I thought I'd go into town,' she said. 'You said the charity shops were good, right?'

'They're the best, so I've been told. Rich pickings from all us oldies pegging out.' He smiled, sadly. She looked down at her phone and typed a message.

'I thought we might walk over the Seven Sisters later. If you fancy. There's a pub. The food's quite good. We could eat dinner there, get a cab back.'

'Sounds good,' she said, typing another message.

'That's decided then.'

The water collecting in the sink was finally clear. He added washing-up liquid and felt arms around him. He turned and her tallness was awkward. Her hair had been fixed into a bun, chopsticks keeping it up, and he worried the points might poke into his cheek. She held on to him and he rubbed her shoulders and the tops of her arms.

'It's okay, it'll all be okay,' he said. He used to say the same to his boy. To Val. He hadn't known what he meant then either.

She stepped away, picked up her phone and smiled. The sun was warming the windows, bright cool light setting off a series of kitchen motes.

He should have asked her. Asked her then and there.

But she was on her way out, and she was calm and healthy, and she had run along the coastal path, from the jetty up to Peacehaven and then back. And ultimately it didn't matter. She was fine and happy. She was grand.

'I'll see you later,' she said.

*

In the junk room he took out the suspension file. He sorted through her letters quickly, taking out those written over the last year. There were four, their envelopes the shade of lemon sherbet. He opened the letters and read. Chronologically, from the first – dated in January – to the one that had arrived three weeks before. Two in black ink, two in blue.

In January she was planning a trip to Dublin with some girlfriends. A hen party. She was apprehensive. She did not like being just one of the girls. She was concerned about dressing up. He'd sent her a cheque to have a drink on him; he'd heard Dublin was expensive. *I hope to write to you more*, her letter said. *Your letters are very special to me. Sometimes it is easy to get caught up in your own life, isn't it? You need to be reminded of what's going on elsewhere.* He remembered that one.

Her next letter thanked him for the cheque and explained she'd had a grand time in Dublin. *Though I must say I can't understand*, she wrote, *why anyone would want to marry at my age. I know you did. I know Dad and Mum did too. But neither are terribly good examples are they? (Sorry!)*

In February there was no letter. In March, she was concerned about exams and had fallen in love with an older man whom he thought might be married. *You would like him (don't I always say that?) but Dad wouldn't be pleased. Not that he ever would be.*

April had no letter, nor May. In early June, there was a letter thanking him for the birthday cheque, the running shirt and the stationery. He had not seen her. (The only thing better than a letter: a parcel.) There was no mention of the older man, no mention of her father. College was going well. College was grand. She and three friends were going to get a flat. The deposits were large. Money was needed. She was looking forward to seeing Ben soon. *Dad has been wonderful. He has given me the money.* He had sent her another cheque. He read the letters again in the bathing chill of the sun. He did not know what he hoped to find in them, but he was reading them for a third time when the doorbell rang.

Charities thought his street something of a soft touch, and bibbed agents holding clipboards knocked seemingly most days. Ben left his letters and padded downstairs. He opened the door but there was no bib or clipboard, just his son, who walked straight past him, through the narrow hallway, into the sitting room.

'I'm sorry I didn't call,' Richard said. 'I should have called, shouldn't I?'

Ben watched him from the still-open door. His son with his hands in his trouser pockets, his son standing in the centre of his living room. His son standing, looking at the Lowry print above the fire.

Richard had never been to his father's house. There had been no illness to drive him there, no emergency. Ben's visit once a year on Anna's birthday was enough for them both. No more invitations were ever extended. When Richard thought of his father, Ben realized, he would imagine the old house. He would be thinking of a younger version of his father, sitting in a house he no longer owned.

Ben watched Richard walk through the sitting room into the kitchen. The air smelled of egg and pork-fat and detergent.

'Would you like tea?' Ben said.

'Yes,' Richard said. 'I'd like some tea. Some tea in one of these old cups. Wow, look at them!' Richard walked over to the drainer and picked up one of the drying cups. 'You could get money for these now. Real money. The kids love 'em. Think they're cute. You should try selling them.'

'You think so?'

Ben watched Richard cross to the fridge and begin to rearrange the fridge magnets. Moving them left and right. Ben had not thought of them as having an order, but they appeared out of sorts in their sudden, new configuration. He turned away and filled the kettle.

Richard dragged back one of the chairs and sat at the table. Next to him, the chair over which Anna's running jacket was draped. Ben watched him touch Anna's running jacket, then the tablecloth, palm down, a wedding ring too wide and bold for his finger. Ben took the teapot from the drainer and began to warm it under the tap.

'Did you ask if she'd told us where she was going?'

'What was that?' Ben said.

'You didn't, did you?' Richard said. He looked through into the living room.

Ben turned off the water and turned to see Richard standing, one hand on the table as though testing its strength.

Ben laughed. 'Oh for goodness' sake,' he said. 'Richard, she's twenty-one years old and—'

'And she lives with me and her mother and had she not, at last, answered one of my calls, had a pang of conscience, we'd all still be sitting there thinking the worst. The very worst. You've seen the television. You know what it's like. And you just didn't think. Didn't think to ask her. Didn't think to say something. Didn't think just to give me a call and let me know that she was here. To ask if everything was okay. Didn't even think enough of me to do that. Though what the hell else I should expect, I don't know.'

The kettle agitated. There was a small pane through which to watch the water rise and level. Ben ignored it and looked out of the window, the heads and the hats, the waves of the sea. He spooned out tea leaves. Three teaspoons: one per person, one for the pot. In town Anna was shopping, trying on dresses, ordering a take-away coffee in a paper cup.

'Why are you here, Richard?' Ben said. 'Really, I mean. You could have just called me if you were so worried—'

'Listen, *Dad*, Anna told me she was here. I said to Sue, I said, "Sue, he'll do the right thing, he'll call. Call in the morning. Send a text or email or something." And she said, "Yes. Yes, darling, he'll do the right thing." And there was no message. And I couldn't sleep and there was no message, no call. Nothing. I said to Sue, "Sue," I said, "he's not going to call, is he?" And she just nodded, because she knew as well as I did you wouldn't bother.'

Later, in bed with the notepad on his knees he wrote to Anna: *Your father is entitled to his own opinion, of course, but I can assure you that there was no malice in my not calling or mentioning your arrival. I was too concerned about you to wonder whether you had contacted him. Your father will believe what he likes. He always has. But you don't have to be as myopic as him.*

Ben placed the teapot on the table.

'I'm sorry,' Ben said. 'I'm sorry that you're upset.'

Ben poured milk into his cup and then tea. He looked at his son. *For some reason*, he wrote in bed, later, *your father is convinced of my badness. For want of a better word. He has listened too long to his mother, ignored me for too long. I fear it is too late for us. Too many years have passed. I will not do him the discourtesy of recounting what he said in the kitchen this afternoon. But it was uncalled for and untrue, this is all you need know.*

'Do you remember,' Richard said, pouring his own tea, 'when we took that day trip to Portsmouth?'

Ben picked up his cup and looked at his son. His son was watching him.

'You don't remember?'

'I forget a lot, Richard—'

'I'm not surprised you don't remember, because we never went,' Richard said. 'I was ten and I wanted to see HMS *Victory*. This ringing any bells? You said you would take me. Just the two of us. The pair of us, driving down to the coast together. Remember that? And then we weren't going. It was such a long way. And you had things to do. And we could go some other time. And you said the same then. I'm sorry you're upset. Not sorry *for* something you've done; but sorry for its effect.'

Ben pushed away his cup. He stood and switched on the lamp under the hood of the oven. It made little difference. He switched on the main lights. Three of the eight halogen bulbs were dead. The empty part of the kitchen was lit as though for a stage.

'Are we going to argue about something that happened forty-odd years ago? Is that why you're here?'

'Do you realize,' Richard said, 'that this is the first time we've been alone in a room together for almost fifteen years? And that this is the first time I've ever seen this place? You know that, don't you?'

Ben said nothing. Richard went back to the fridge magnets. The lights hummed slightly.

'Would you like some cake, I have—'

'No I don't want any fucking cake.'

'I don't know what you want from me, Richard. I was concerned only for Anna. She's a grown woman, she doesn't need to run everything past you, you know. You were always like this, even as a child. Had to know everyone's business—'

'I read your letters,' he said. He laughed. 'Oh yes. All the letters you sent to Anna. Did you know that? She left them lying around. She wanted me to read them, I think. So I read them all. What nice handwriting you have. And what a selective memory!'

The stories, the tales of his son. Yes. So many in those letters. How the son that Ben had treated with such love had betrayed him so. How this son had so relished the breakdown of his mother and father's marriage. How he had revelled in telling his father about his mother's new-found happiness with a civil engineer, how his son had barred any real relationship with Anna. How this cruelty had affected Ben, how though he was not angry with this son, he was incapable of being so, he remained wounded every day by his behaviour. They were such good, such truthful letters.

Ben smiled at his son, big and broad.

'You knew?' Richard asked. 'You knew?'

Later that night, with the notepad on his knees Ben wrote: *Your father now believes that my letters are little more than poison directed at him, through you. How was I to know that he would betray your trust and read your personal letters? How was I to know that he would be so invasive? All I have tried to do is be honest about my past, and my present, give you, perhaps, the benefit of my experiences. Also perhaps an understanding of why your father is the way that he is.*

The doorbell rang. Ben got up and let Anna in. She had

three bags: Cancer Research, British Heart Foundation, Scope. She saw her father and put down the bags. She kissed her grandfather on the cheek.

'Has he been here long?' she said.

'Hello, love. We've been—'

'What did I tell you?' Anna said, turning towards her father. 'You promised you'd leave me alone. You promised.'

The two of them argued. Loud and quiet, mad and silent. *These are the days of miracle and wonder.* Ben watched as he melted into the furniture, as ignored as a hat-stand. Anna calling her father a controlling, manipulative, hateful man. Anna pointing her finger and Richard trying to interrupt without success. Anna telling him that she was never coming home and would never live with him again. That he was a terrible father and a terrible man without a shred of dignity. There was tea left in the pot and Ben poured some out into his cup, listening to the consistency and heat of Anna's anger. He watched his son say no, you don't understand, I never meant, and lose his temper and accuse her of being a terrible daughter, a burden on her mother, on the whole family. Selfish, arrogant. And he watched Anna say, me? Arrogant, coming from you? And Ben sipped his cooling tea and watched them as their voices grew louder and louder, his son's face becoming redder, and he wondered if his son would be able to keep his anger checked. Ben watched his son throw a teacup at the wall.

'Get out,' Anna said. 'Get out of this house now.'

Richard looked at his daughter, and then at his father. Ben smiled.

'Go on,' Anna said. 'Out.'

She pushed him. His son. Richard. Anna pushed her father and he put his arms up. He looked at his father. Ben smiled. Richard left the house; his car leaving quickly.

Ben looked at the smashed cup. Ben looked at Anna, crying.

'You sit down,' Ben said. 'Anna, you sit down and I'll clean all of this up.'

WINGS

In the parlour window her face is reflected; behind it a photograph of an extended forearm, gothic script running from elbow to wrist: *Only God Can Judge Me*. The photograph is laminated, its edges bleached by sunlight, but the tattoo's ink remains a deep greenblack, the surrounding skin a tight, painful red. She looks away, to the pavement, then back to the other photographs.

A back-bound Madonna; a blood-wristed Christ on a well-built pectoral; a knifed skull ablaze on an upper thigh; a young man's neck, the tattoo beginning at the lobe of his left ear and ending at his clavicle. No faces shown.

She'd once known a man with a swallow inked on his neck; he'd bothered them both: yes. Her and Gwen. Years ago now, in a pub that no longer exists. The pair of them laughing as they ran away, the tattooed man shouting the names they'd invented from the doorway.

The bell rings, last-orders-like, as she enters. Two men behind a scrubbed chrome counter, arms like advertisements, play cards for matchsticks. The turn of the next card determines who will rise and greet Maria. The card falls and the thinner of the two – neatly bearded, ear-ringed, a Hawaiian shirt over the tattoos – rises from his chair.

'Can I help?' he says.

'I hope so,' she says. 'I was wondering. Do I need an appointment? Or can you fit me in now?'

'That all depends,' he says. 'Depends entirely on what you want.'

'I want wings,' she says. 'I want a pair of wings on my back, just here.'

With her thumb, she points to her shoulder blade and catches her reflection in the mirrored walls; posed, her thumb out, like hitching a lift, disastrous camping holiday, Scotland, 1991.

'Wings?' he says.

'Yes,' she says. 'Wings.'

*

This is how she has imagined it:

Tattooist: Listen, lady – *the tattooist's voice is American, Deep South, Alabama perhaps* – wings are a lot a ink. You can't have 'em small, can you, Hutch?

The other tattooist shakes his head and sucks on a straw spiked into a Big Gulp cup.

Maria: I'm aware of that – *her speaking voice has*

become icy British, just at the public-school end of Received Pronunciation – I've done my research. Can I see your designs, please?

Tattooist: We do about fifteen different kinds a wing. Which kind were you thinking? You have a picture or something?

Maria: No. I'd just like to see the designs, please.

Tattooist: No picture?

Maria: Just show me the wings.

Tattooist: I ain't showing you nothing, lady.

Maria: I have money—

Tattooist: It ain't about the money, lady. Same thing happened to a buddy a mine. This stuck-up chick comes into his parlour, she hands over her black Amex card and he inks her. Month later she's suing him for taking advantage of her *weakened psychological state*. You see what I'm saying?

Maria bristles at the grammatical confusion.

Maria: It's my sister's birthday. My sister, Gwen. She would have been forty today – *Maria takes two thousand pounds from her handbag and places it on the counter. It is a paper-bound brick like those used in exchange for kidnapped children* – this is important.

The tattooist says nothing and takes out a large port-folio from under the desk, stops on a page and turns it to face Maria. The page is full of wings. He points his finger at a design in the bottom right-hand corner. It is hand-drawn, beautiful; two small wings just as she imagined them.

Tattooist: They're the only ones I'll ink. Not too big, not too detailed, fine for when you want them removed.

Maria: I'm never going to have them removed – *she puts her hand over the image, strokes the design* – they're perfect. Just perfect.

*

It is nothing like she imagined. There are over sixty different pairs of wings in the portfolio and the tattooist is all too helpful in picking out a design. Many come with a little background, a summary of how long they take to ink, whether he feels it is a good design for her. It reminds her of looking at carpet swatches and kitchen counter tops she couldn't afford; salesmen pitching the longevity, the luxury of their product. Like those men, the tattooist repeats that *at the end of the day* the choice is hers. She sees so many pairs inked on so many backs she develops a kind of wing blindness. They blur and flounder, seem ready to stretch and flap away.

By the turn of the fifth page, she understands that no one will tell her no. No one is going to find her mental health wanting, refuse her payment, finally ask for someone else's permission. Who would be able to grant such permission, anyway? Would there need to be a consensus of friends and family as a safeguard against such action? Or references, perhaps? Would she be forced to forge her husband's signature? In his handwriting state: I have been married to Maria Carlton for sixteen years and I can confirm that she has always wanted and admired tattoos?

Maria momentarily notices herself in the mirrors: the stiffness of her clothes, the age-appropriate hairstyle, the messy casualness of a working mother, the redness around her eyes.

'My sister died,' she says as he points to a pair of wings that cover the entirety of a man's back. 'It's her birthday today.'

'A tattoo's a good way to remember someone,' he says. 'The earliest tattoos were for remembrance, you know?'

He sticks out his forearm and in amongst the swirls and curlicues are a man's name, a date of birth and a date of death, roses like bindweed surrounding the lettering.

'She said, Gwen that is, my younger sister, she said that when she was forty we'd both get tattoos. Both of us,' Maria says as the tattooist turns the page again. 'So, here I am. Alone, but not, if you see what I'm saying.'

'Yes. So you are,' he says, and turns the portfolio fully to Maria.

'These,' he says tapping the bottom right of the page. 'These ones.'

It is a pencil-drawn image on tracing paper, thin and brittle grey. The wings are delicate and subtle; spindly lines, slightly crooked, suggestive rather than fully downed and feathered: still able to pinch at her shoulder blades though, still able to beat and lift her into the night air.

'What do you think?' he says.

'Gwen would have loved them.'

'Gwen doesn't have to live with them,' he says. He smiles and they share a small laugh; a moment's warmth and understanding.

'I want them,' she says. 'They're perfect.'

'I'm glad,' he says. 'So, okay. Just a couple of things to go through before we get started.'

He picks up a sheet of A4 from both of the wire-mesh baskets under the counter. He asks her to read and sign them and she scans them in panic. They are nothing to worry about, some legal documentation and certifications of consent. Still, her signatures on the dotted lines are not her own. She writes Gwen's name instead. The other tattooist asks if she would like something to drink.

'Wine, if you have it,' she says. 'Red wine.'

'I was thinking more of coffee, or perhaps a tea. No booze, you see,' he says shaking his head. 'It's against the law.'

'Don't be such a spoilsport,' the other tattooist says. 'I can get some wine from upstairs if you really want some.'

'It's all right,' the other man says, 'I'll go.'

She watches him disappear through a door, no doubt calling a friend as he lumbers up the stairs – *you'll never guess what* – beginning a dissection of the woman taking off her working clothes, hanging up her jacket and blouse, wrapping a towel around herself and lying front-ways on the large black tattooing chair.

The tattooist's fingers are thin and cold on her back; he talks and she remembers to reply. There is music softly playing and beneath that the softer hum of the ink gun and even lower, even softer than that, once he begins, the pain. The pain is inconstant. As the wings begin to take shape, she concentrates on the buzzing etch of the needle and the brief pauses while he wipes away her blood.

Maria should be thinking about Gwen, about the house they shared and the promises they made; but instead she is thinking about distance, about why some things feel near and some far away, and about the kind of person who would want *Only God Can Judge Me* tattooed on his arm; and how the moments you tell yourself always to remember are just as easily forgotten as those you don't.

She opens her eyes and sees the wine glass and the mirrored glimpse of the tattooist at work, then closes them again and thinks of Gwen – thankfully, finally – and the time they hired a pedalo with the last of their money, and in the darkening pond drove that boat in furious circles.

Gwen had come to stay, a few days no more, and had remained there for a couple of years. Four years younger, not the sense she was born with, according to their father, just twenty then and working in a clothes shop by day, out on the town in the evening. Maria was in and out of work, a supply cover here, a maternity cover there, never quite getting the nod to stay on, never quite holding on.

'Fuck 'em,' Gwen would say. 'Fuck 'em all.' And her plan would be a night out, a bar, a club, a place that Maria would wish to leave early, wanting only to head for her sofa, for her bed, to sleep, to rest. Gwen would insist, she was persuasive in a way that was impossible to resist. The pedalo had been her idea. Never mind the money. Money always sorts itself out. Her long hair with the jagged fringe, protruding hips, wide angry mouth. Leather jacket and short skirts, cigarettes and eyeliner, pub breath and a stare that invited all manner of interpretations.

The four-year difference in age was acute when they were young, Maria calling Gwen her little teddy bear until Gwen was six. Gwen though grew quickly, in height, in demeanour, in personality. She could darken a room with entry, or lighten it, depending on mood. The house they shared – though nominally Maria's – became her space, her domain. When eventually Maria moved out to be with Tom, Gwen stayed on, a co-worker from the shop taking the vacant room. Maria found visiting difficult, like looking into her unlived life.

When the diagnosis came, it was Maria who needed the calming, the support. Gwen leapt the five stages and headed straight to acceptance. Gwen would not move out of the flat. Gwen still headed out into the city night, still told her sister to lighten up. And then she was in the hospital, her family surrounding her, facing it all down with smiles and flashes of her stained, small teeth.

As the hum and buzz and wipe finishes, Maria is thinking of the conversation about tattoos. They were sitting in the lounge, Maria out of work again, two bottles of cheap red wine on the cracked coffee table. She can hear her sister, but she's only watching her. The way she paces, the way she wrinkles her nose sometimes, the sheer annoyed-joy of being in the same room as her, of appearing in the same frame. She thinks of blowing out a single candle in an individual Bakewell tart. Make a wish. That birthday smell of extinguished wick. Make a wish.

'All done,' the tattooist says. 'You can take a look now.'

Maria bunches the towel to her chest as she gets up, sore and feeling the burn of the needle and ink. She allows the tattooist to position her so she can see his work. On her shoulder blades, she has wings. Light, delicate, almost moth-like wings. She can feel them pulling at her, ready to flutter and flap.

'Thank you,' she says.

The tattooist asks her questions, but she looks only at her back, at the wings newly there. She watches her wings spread stiffly in the cold afternoon light. The tattooist asks more questions, but she does not answer them.

'They're perfect,' is all she says. 'They're just perfect.'

*

During the first week she dresses and undresses in the dark, the wings safely hidden beneath pyjamas or working clothes. When people touch her, however briefly, she feels the pulse of their suspicion. Seven days of discomfort in Tom's morning clinch, of short temper with the girls, of quickly closed doors. In the bathroom, as often as she can, she removes her clothes and examines the wings, pulls the skin taut over her shoulder blades. She does not think of Gwen as she does this. Not at all. Reflected in a mirror, her wings look bigger, more complicated.

On the fifteenth day she is teaching a year-eleven class. It is the opening lesson of the day, normally the best time for getting through unscathed, but that morning they are already restless. She has moved Chas to the front and he sits there looking at her, in his face something she has not seen before.

'What's that?' Maria says as something is passed from Dre to Sandip.

'Nothing, Miss,' Dre says.

Maria strides down the aisle and plucks the note from under the boy's hand.

The note says *I so wanna fuck Miss C so bad.* It is Chas's handwriting. Maria puts it in her pocket and returns to the whiteboard, runs through the equation and its solution, unsure whether the burn of her face or the burn from her wings is more intense. She looks at the note throughout the day to check it hasn't changed. She has been teaching since she was twenty-two and she has never provoked such a reaction. There has always been another teacher to take the heat.

The note is in her pocket as she drives to the child-minder. Maria waves at the woman and her youngest, Amy, bundles towards the car, all bag and coat, perfectly red-round blushes on her cheeks. Chloe, twelve and still insulted she has not been entrusted with her sibling's safety, ambles behind. They get in the car and both, today, kiss her.

'Hello,' Maria says. 'You two had a good day?'

'Yes, Mum,' they say not quite in turn, not quite in unison.

'Me too,' she says.

'You look pretty today,' Amy says as they drive away.

'You're not getting a puppy,' Maria says. 'I've told you before and I'll tell you again, you're not getting a puppy.'

Amy looks slightly perplexed. The note burns shamefully in Maria's pocket.

'Actually, Mum, you do look good at the moment,' says Chloe. 'She's right, for once.'

'That's very sweet of you both,' she says and checks her reflection in the rear-view mirror. She does not see any difference, her face still too wide and plump, haircut too severe, eyes thin and heavy. She imagines the wings throbbing, or perhaps they do. All the way home she can't decide.

Once the girls are in bed and Tom is reading Harry Potter to Amy, she lies on the sofa in front of two glasses of wine. There is a programme paused on the television and she is finishing off the last of her marking. In his exercise book, Chas's algebraic a, b and cs remind her of the note. It has been on her mind anyway, working through the books, knowing his would be there in the stack. Gwen would have humiliated that boy. She would have made him an example, shown the girls in class that they did not need to accept this kind of behaviour. Her sister would have found it hilarious; would have asked her whether she was going to pursue it.

'Boys are at their sexual peak at that age,' she'd have said. 'You should make up for your prudish youth!'

A prudish youth: yes. Even when she and Gwen lived together. Tom the first and last. Toilet-brush hair and stupid jokes and the look and sound of a posh boy. And even that first time, when it was over, he'd held her tight as swaddling. He held her all the night and into the morning. She never felt him letting go.

Tom opens the lounge door, and with the exaggerated steps of Wile E. Coyote tiptoeing away from one of his own bombs, he joins her on the sofa. Tom has long spindly legs that add to the effect. She laughs even though she has seen it a thousand times.

'Levity? Laughter?' he says. 'On a Tuesday? With *your* reputation?'

'You bring it out in me,' she says and picks up her wine glass.

Something flashes, glints, and her hand freezes as she's still holding the wine; a thought that needs to be spooled back.

Tom smiles. He rubs her feet, left and right, and she relaxes again and puts down the wine. He presses play and the programme begins with the pursuit of a young girl, the scene shot with jagged, hand-held camera work. The opening credits roll. She looks at the wine glass on the coffee table and realizes she hasn't thought of Gwen once today. Not once. Always she thinks of her. Perhaps unlatching the morning door, clothed from a night out.

Maybe brushing her hair, picking her toenails on the sofa. Perhaps turning channels on the television, maybe giving some sage, useless advice. But today, nothing.

Without thinking she reaches for the remote and turns off the television. She puts her hand on his and kisses deep into the crevice of his neck.

'I want to go to bed,' she says. His hand feels cumbersome beneath hers. As she pulls him up she can feel resistance, not a little confusion.

'Come now,' she says.

The bedroom is dark at her insistence; for this function it is always dark. After long kisses, she feels his hands on her back, palms on the wings, fingers massaging where the ink has stained and he does not seem to notice anything different. The ease of this deception surprises her. She lies down on the bed, sweat on her top lip, her illustrated skin sticking to the fitted bed sheet, but otherwise entirely airborne.

They make love every night that week. When the pleasure comes, she feels the wings beating, taking her higher, up into darkness. Tom is excited by the freedom she allows. He touches her bottom in public, kisses her open-mouthed in front of the girls. This is what it feels like to be desired; what it is to desire.

*

Good fortune stalks her. Tom at last finds a job; pay okay, enough for them to breathe easier, tackle some of the debts. She receives a pay rise and a school inspection records good things about her teaching. The kids, hers and the ones in class, behave. Amy is accepted on a scholarship to the local public school and Chloe is given the kind of glowing report that the year before would have seemed impossible. In class, Maria senses trouble before it happens, hears the jokes before they are told, sees the tears before students weep. At home, the girls seem to listen to her a little more closely; do not shy away when she gathers them into her arms. Tom and Maria redecorate and have people over for dinner; both of them cook. Everyone – Kevin and Megan, Alex and Helen, John and Nick – agrees that the house looks lovely; that they have done so much with the space.

She thinks of Gwen at random moments. She is there at school – walking the corridors, red-lipsticked, bobbles on her thick black tights, legs *like pipe-cleaners*, a rucked-up skirt – but mostly she is there when Maria is alone, in front of the mirror.

Maria wonders whether Gwen would have forgotten about the tattoos by the time of her fortieth birthday. Wonders whether she only has such a fearsomely exact memory of the poorly carpeted flat, the wood-box television set, the garish print above the mantel salvaged from a skip, and the promise made that they would get tattoos because Gwen never even saw her thirtieth birthday. Had she lived, would Gwen have questioned it ever having happened? *I said that? Really? I don't remember that. Maybe I did. I talked the most perfect rubbish then.*

*

The house is silent and Maria is in her bedroom, shirtless and looking over her shoulder, pulling the skin taut over her shoulder blades. The morning is bright and the windows are open, curtains too. She looks at the tattoo and is glad it is Saturday morning.

Maria woke after Tom and the girls had headed out; a cup of tea left for her on the bedside table. Every Saturday the same, Tom taking the kids swimming. He swims alone, lengths, while the girls take classes with a trained coach. Maria never swims, only occasionally watches her daughters from the observation area, high up, the chlorine stink giving her headaches. She hates swimming pools.

She is thankful for the quiet, though the argument of the previous night remains loud.

'Won't you think of the girls?' he'd said. 'Won't you think of me?'

That night he'd come home in excitement. An old colleague had moved to Orlando and had offered him their condominium there, they could stay for free. There was a pool. Huge and blue. They could swim; they could go to Disney World. It would be the first time they'd all gone abroad.

She thought of the wings. She thought of the pool. She shook her head.

'I'm never getting on an aeroplane,' she said. 'You can't make me. You know how scared I am of flying.'

They had tried to convince her. They had failed. She said the fear was too great. The wings twitched every time she said she would not fly. They twitched with every untruth.

It is the girls she thinks of as she observes the spreading, rousant wings on her back. When eventually she tells them of the wings, they will be delighted; they will trace their fingers over them; ask to hang on to her legs as she ascends. Her wings give a small shiver; she has been busy and has neglected them: she is glad to see them now in all their strength, in all their intricacy on her shoulder blades.

The girls were born after Gwen died, though Chloe has developed a considerable interest in her namesake – Tom would not have Gwen as a first name, so they sandwiched it between Chloe and Carlton. From photograph albums, Chloe has extracted the pictures of Gwen, the unpleasant gloss of the late eighties, the bad skin and badly cropped hair, and tacked them to the noticeboard in the girls' shared bedroom. Chloe asks Maria about her sister often, and already understands she is being given the barest minimum, only a partial truth.

In the mirror the wings look as though they have always been there. Maria thinks of Gwen, un-illustrated, and begins to heave from the stomach, crying without tears. A kind of not-crying, a sort of anti-crying. She sits down on the edge of the bed and puts her head in her hands and imagines her sister laughing. The intensity of it spangles. The wings beat and she opens her eyes to see her sister standing in the mirror, staring at her, eyes fixed and dilated. Maria smiles at her sister, and there is no Gwen, just Chloe, her daughter, with red eyes and wet hair.

Chloe is open-mouthed. Maria wants to say something but does not.

'Holy shit,' Chloe says. 'Holy shit. Dad!'

Chloe stares at the wings, Maria closes her eyes. Soon Tom is at the door, paternal hands on Chloe's shoulders, turning her away and onto the small landing.

'Go to your room,' he says quietly and Chloe does as she's told, though her mouth is open, desperate to speak. Tom walks back into their bedroom and closes the door. It is a small room, a double bed that doesn't quite stretch as far as his legs, a wardrobe badly bolted to the wall, an inherited dressing table: far from the room he'd imagined for them. He looks at Maria's wings, looks at the room. They will need money to move.

The conversation they should be having is about this. About affording a new house, giving the girls a room each now Chloe's first period announced itself at the pool. He should be saying: *We knew this day was coming soon.* He should be saying to her now: *We knew they couldn't share a room for ever.* It should be the conversation for which they'd once prepared themselves, laughing at what it would be like with teenagers when both of them felt like teenagers themselves. He should be saying: *We'll get through this.*

Her shoulders are rounded, the tattooed wings lithe. He sits at a right angle to her; his hand on her back, just below the ink.

'I see you've been hiding something from me,' he says.

The wings are huge. Angels', he thinks, with licks of what might be flame, though without colour it's hard to be sure. They look large enough to support flight.

'It's almost funny,' Tom says. 'I could laugh. Seriously, I could laugh.'

He starts to trace the outline of the wings, then stops.

'What else have you been hiding from me?' he says. 'What else have you got tattooed? You haven't got a T and an M, one on each buttock, have you?'

In her class she's seen how laughter can soon become the baying of a mob. She hears the same keening in Tom's voice now, feels the people behind him, pointing where he points.

She sees him in the dressing-table mirrors; the three panels showing different aspects of his face: thin and greyly pinched. She can smell the pool on him, a scent that gathers as he gets up quickly from the bed. He is looking at the door, the pillows, the rug.

'Are you not going to say anything?' he says. 'Are you not going to say anything at all?'

'I won't apologize,' she says. 'I made a promise. I made a promise to Gwen.'

She looks at him in defiance: yes. He is shaking his head and staring at the wings' reflection. He kneels down and his hands come for her face, her cheeks between penitent hands.

'You told me you wouldn't do anything like this again,' Tom says. 'You swore it to me, remember?'

'I said I'd never do anything that affects us all without telling you beforehand,' she says. 'This is about me. Me and no one else.'

There is a kind of pleading, but for what she cannot say. Her breath is fast and shallow. He shakes his head and removes his hands from her face. He stands and looks down on her until she's standing too. She holds out her hands, *come now*. He lists for a moment and then folds his arms around her. In the mirror, he can see his hands on her wings. His fingers on the tips, palms small against their span. He can hear the girls talking and fighting; Chloe is saying terrible things. Chloe is saying things that are making Amy cry.

'It's only my body,' Maria says. 'That's all, it's only my body. My body, isn't it?'

'We'll get through this,' Tom says. 'We will.'

'It's only my body,' she says. 'It's only my body, isn't it?' she says.

The two girls are fighting. Tom looks at the wings. He holds them as they shake, as they shrug from the tears.

'Yes, Maria,' he says. 'Yes, it's only your body.'

SOMETHING ELSE TO SAY

The Tap has twenty-seven beers on draught. Twenty-seven beers on draught and only one toilet. This is something to say. Yes. And the toilet is upstairs, at the top of a spiral staircase. This is something else to say. A follow-up. There is a third thing to say, too: you wouldn't have thought it would be allowed, what with Health & Safety and all that. And the beer, of course. Twenty-seven different kinds to sample and discuss. Four, then. Four things to say.

The Tap is a renovated Portland stone lodge south of Euston railway station. It has a squared horseshoe bar with space only for stools and standing, the twenty-seven beers named and numbered on a chalkboard above. When ordering use the name of the beer, or part thereof, never the number. Remember: you are served better if you ask for a recommendation. There are tables upstairs, but they are too close to the single, solitary toilet. The Tap has twenty-seven beers on draught and only one toilet.

As I walked in there were four things to say. Four.

There was a man behind the bar and a man sitting on a stool to his right. He was finishing a pint of dark, almost black beer. He wore battle fatigues. Sand camouflage – Iraq, Afghanistan, those kinds of places – heavy, polished boots. He wore a wedding ring; in front of him a newspaper open at the gossip pages. His hair was grey, his stubble dashed with white, wrinkles like knife marks on clay. Too old for the army. Surely too old. Too old to be a ground trooper. To fight. Surely.

'Another?' the barman asked.

'No,' the army man said. The army man stood and picked up his old kitbag: *smile, smile, smile*. He walked past me, walked straight past me without acknowledgement. Like the changing of the guard, of the watch. An old kitbag, an open newspaper, an empty beer glass. A fifth thing to say. Yes.

'When I got here there was a man wearing battle fatigues. Full battle fatigues, but he looked much too old to be a soldier. How old do you reckon you have to be before you have to stop fighting?' Five things to say. The last one a question. A conversation starter. Good.

Above the bar, numbers fifteen to twenty-three had no corresponding beer. Chalk ghosts of percentage signs and names and prices were smudged on the slate. Remember: you are served better if you ask for a recommendation.

'What can I get you, mate?' the barman asked.

'What would you recommend?'

The barman was young. Bearded, friendly faced. There was nothing to say about him. He turned to the chalkboard, put a hand to his beard, looked at the empty spaces where beers fifteen to twenty-three should have been. Whichever beer the barstaff recommend, they always say it's quite hoppy. Hops are in fashion. Rish had told me this. He'd pointed this out years ago. Five things to say. Five.

'Well, how about Independence?' the barman said. 'It's quite hoppy.'

He served me a taster in a shot glass: all head, a liquid hit at the end. I nodded in appreciation, the way Rish had shown me. The barman poured me a full glass. I wondered what number Independence would be when it was eventually slated. I guessed twenty-one. For some reason I thought: *21, Kelly's Eye*. The bingo call. But Kelly's Eye is one. Twenty-one is Key of the Door. I thanked the barman and paid. Five things to say.

Sitting at a stool by the window, I looked up Kelly's Eye on my telephone. Its derivation. Military slang; possibly a reference to Ned Kelly. This is good trivia. Nice fit with the army man, too. A continuation. Five things to say. No, six. Twenty-seven beers and only one toilet; the toilet is up narrow stairs; you wouldn't have thought it would be allowed; the man in battle fatigues; Kelly's

Eye. And the beer. Yes, the beer. The Independence. Quite hoppy. Yes.

Outside, a delivery from the Five Points brewery was in progress. It was around 12.15pm and I had six things to say. Behind me the barman was on a stepladder, writing the names of the beers in chalk. Good, steady hand. I watched each one with interest until Independence came in at nineteen. There is no bingo call for nineteen. I discovered this from the Kelly's Eye page. No bingo call for nineteen, but there is for fourteen. The Lawnmower. This is good trivia. Fourteen is the lawnmower because lawnmowers have a fourteen-inch blade. This is not something to say. Too much bingo trivia. Six things to say. Six.

*

Waiting should never be advertised. Even to those for whom you are waiting. Ideally, the arrival of a companion should occur when one is so immersed in something else that one jolts when he or she says hello. I thought this exactly in those words. It sounded pompous. I thought it again, as spoken by James Mason. I looked up James Mason on my telephone. He was born in Huddersfield. This was glorious: Rish would be delighted. There is nothing better than an unexpected Yorkshireman. This is something to say. Seven things to say. Seven.

I took out a book to read. Do not read a newspaper,

it looks like waiting. Crosswords doubly so. There was a bookmark: a train ticket. I read three sentences from the centre of the right-hand page, went forward three sentences, back three sentences, but nothing looked familiar. I tried the left-hand page. Nothing there either. I flicked forward and back. Nothing seemed familiar. I find that with reading. I am a skipper. A jumper. I lack concentration.

The book's spine was cracked, its cover torn; there were ink smudges on the page ends. He may well comment on it. *I see you still can't take care of a book.* Yes. *You always make them look like something smuggled out from a Bangkok prison.* Give him something to talk about first. Clever. I set it down on the shelf under the window next to my pint glass. I couldn't mention it, though; it would seem forced. Still, seven things to say.

From the window seat I watched the exit and entrance to Euston bus terminus, beyond that, the railway station. People walked past and no one looked like Rish.

*

New York City, midtown in late-February, a bar called the Ginger Man, sauerkraut and sausages, Victory Pilsner, afternoon drinks with the promise of an evening over on the Upper East Side with friends of Rosemary, sounds like a euphemism and in some ways it is, the look on Rish's face and in his eyes, below a haircut, subtly fashionable, the strong accent still, Whitby, Dracula country, and a new way of ending a meal with a dab of a napkin to the mouth, three guys walking through the door, proper Jews, forelocks and everything, Rish talking about some jerk at work, his rhyming words, and the Jews ordering their beers from the menu, hundreds on draught, and the barman serving the drinks in frosted mugs and Rish smiling, his teeth not yet American, and saying he's got something to tell me, and I already know what he's going to tell me because I arrived the night before and Rosemary elegantly dodged wine with dinner, and through that smile, its wattage, he tells me the news, his news, and we embrace in the post-work rush and the server takes our order for more expensive beer and we toast the unborn, may your first child be a masculine child, Luca Brasi, and Rosemary arrives soon afterwards, work suit and heels you can hear and she looks older – perhaps it's the pregnancy – and she says to me *don't say it* and I say *what?* and she says *you know*, and I say *what?* and she says *don't say it* and all I can think to say is *Rosemary's Baby, Rosemary's Baby, Rosemary's Baby*, but I say nothing and when she goes to the toilet – there are hundreds of toilets at the Ginger Man, this is America and there would never just be one toilet – I realize I've never seen the film *Rosemary's Baby*, and don't really know what it's about, and Rosemary comes back and we toast her health with the Virgin Mary that the waitress has brought over and Rosemary's accent is perfect, screen-goddess American, and Rish's accent is Yorkshire, ee-by-gum Yorkshire and my accent is all over the place and I am drunk from the Victory Pilsner and there are three of them and one of me and New York's a-go-go and every drink tastes nice, and they talk about the apartment they will move to, their parents – her parents, let's be quite clear about this – helping them get somewhere bigger than the shoe-box apartment they rent above a Brazilian restaurant in Chelsea, and we are clinking glasses and may their first child be a masculine child, Luca Brasi, and there are three of them and one of me, three of them and one of me.

*

His reflection in the window. Twenty-seven beers and one toilet; the toilet is up narrow stairs; you wouldn't have thought it would be allowed; a man in battle fatigues; Kelly's Eye; James Mason. And the beer. Twenty-seven different kinds. And his reflection in the window. He put his hand on my shoulder. I turned and smiled and stood and we embraced for a moment longer than necessary or normal, then a moment more than that, then a moment more. Then we broke.

Rish had lost a little weight from his face. He was

red-eyed and his skin was flawed with squeezed spots. He smelled of the same aftershave he always wore. There was grey at his temples. Standard issue, stress related.

'How was the flight?' I asked. He only had a small bag. A kind of businessman's overnight case. He stowed it under the shelf. I had forgotten this was something to say. A question to ask. Your mind works on such things even when you don't realize it.

'Dreadful,' Rish said. 'Never fly American. I say it every time, but I never listen. Seriously, you'd be better off walking. Never again. What we drinking?'

'Independence,' I said. 'It's quite hoppy. You try.'

I passed him my glass. He took a sip and passed back the glass. Made the appreciation face.

'It's quite hoppy,' he said. 'You want the same again?'

'No,' I said. Never order the same beer twice. Even if you enjoyed the first. Even if none of the others appeal, you must try something different.

'I'll have a Triangle,' I said. Number fourteen. The Lawnmower.

'You got it, son.' His accent terrible. Yorkshire via New York.

The barman climbed down from the stepladder, wiped his hands on a towel. I watched Rish sample three different beers: nine, thirteen, twenty-six. You can sample up to three, no more than that: this is the unwritten rule.

I watched him take a tiny glass, give his appreciation face, move on to the next. I wished for no victor. For Rish to shake his head, the unwritten rule be damned, and ask for three more to taste. I wanted the barman to line up a sample of each beer and for Rish to begin at number one and end at twenty-seven, compile a longlist of ten, taste them again and announce a shortlist of six, then decide upon the final winner. He went for twenty-six. I had gambled on nine.

Their child caught a disease. One of those with a name that can stop the heart. It was an aggressive strain. Three months and then. This is the stuff you can't even think. Cannot comprehend. There were photographs of the funeral. They looked professionally taken. Well framed and composed. Rish emailed them to me. Rish accepted my apologies. I couldn't get the time. Didn't have the money. Would have done anything. Understand, yes? They named the boy Noah. I'd held him in the living room of my house, in a restaurant, in the beer garden of a pub. He had cried and smiled and shit and gurgled. He wore a jumper I'd bought. Red, knitted Adidas logo. Loved that jumper. One week there, one week back in England. Two weeks I knew him. I cannot remember his face, the way he felt in my arms, his weight. I can remember his smell. I can remember his skin.

After the funeral. Months after, not so long, Rosemary

and Rish split up. In an Indian restaurant she threw a chana dhal at him and said it was over. Men and women process guilt and mourning differently. He told me this on the phone. Calling from the Chelsea Holiday Inn. Drunk yes, drunk and like he was reading out from a fucking manual or something.

Rosemary moved to be with her parents upstate. Like Russian dolls, a mother retreating to her girlhood bedroom. Rish got drunk for two weeks and did something with a college girl. He told me this in shame. Calling from Chelsea Holiday Inn. Reassuring me it was okay, he was okay. He'd be home soon. Not to worry. Home soon.

Rish came back with the drinks. He sat down and looked out of the window.

'They've got twenty-seven beers on draught,' I said. 'But only one toilet.'

'What's that?' he said.

'I said they've got twenty-seven beers on draught,' I said again. 'But only one toilet.'

'Really?' he said.

He was forty-one. A father and a husband; neither now and both. A father and a husband looking out of a pub window at 12.17pm on a Wednesday.

'Yes,' I said. 'And the toilet's up those really narrow stairs.'

I pointed to the staircase.

'You wouldn't have thought it would be allowed, would you? What with Health & Safety and all that?'

Rish looked at the stairs. I was going too quickly. One, two and three had been used up without Rish even really hearing.

'What did you go for in the end?' I asked.

'Conqueror,' he said. 'Quite hoppy. You try?'

I took his glass and took a sip.

'Yes, nice,' I said.

He nodded and looked out of the window again. Were there six or seven things to say? Seven. Four gone. Only three things left to say. The man in fatigues. Kelly's Eye. James Mason.

'Yes,' I said. 'It's quite hoppy, isn't it?'

'Honestly, I mean it,' he said. 'American really is the worst. BA, Virgin, even Delta – anyone but them.'

The stool made a wounded scraping sound as he moved it. This would be his advice for years; forever probably. *So you're going to New York? Don't fly American. Trust me.* And they would trust him because everyone trusted Rish, and when they booked flights they would remember what he'd said and pay a little more to avoid American. And they would parrot the information Rish gave – *well, a friend of mine used to live out there and he said never fly American* – and they wouldn't understand that he would never go back.

'You grew a beard,' he said and smiled.

'I don't like it,' I said. 'It's a bit ginger in places.'

'Why don't you shave it off then?'

'Because it took commitment and now I have it, it's like a war of attrition.'

'It suits you,' he said. 'It looks good.'

The barman turned on the stereo. Playlist, same as always, always on random. It was Cream. 'Sunshine of Your Love'. Rish looked out of the window and I looked out of the window with him. We saw buses and buggies and taxi-cabs and women wearing vest tops and baseball caps. There is a guitar solo on 'Sunshine of Your Love'. Clapton plays the opening bars of 'Blue Moon': a moon to contrast with the sunshine. I knew this. Something else to say. Eight things to say. Four down, four to go.

'Did you know,' I said, 'that this guitar solo is actually the opening to "Blue Moon"?'

'Really?' he said.

'Yes. "Blue Moon". You can hear it clearly,' I said. 'Listen.'

We sat in silence listening to the guitar line. Our heads in the air, as though we could catch the notes.

'There's a beer called Blue Moon,' Rish said. 'They serve it with a wedge of orange. It's disgusting. And it's owned by fucking Coors or something.'

'I've had Blue Moon,' I said. 'You're right, it's horrible, yes.'

Two men in suits came in. Pinstripes and knitted ties. I saw them in the window. Heard them. Loud voices talking about something. They interrupted their conversation to order a twenty and a number four, then resumed their loud talk. Rish finished his drink.

'I'm going to have a Redemption next,' Rish said. Redemption is the name of the beer. Look it up. There's no irony there, that's the name of the beer he wanted.

'I'll get them,' I said and took his glass to the bar.

'What'll it be?' the barman said.

'Can I try the Citra?' I said. 'And perhaps the Big Chief?'

The sun came in thick bars through the window, then disappeared. Rish was still looking out of the window. The barman poured and set down the shots. They tasted identical. There was Kelly's Eye. There was the military man. There was James Mason. Three things left to say.

Rish nodded in thanks and sipped at his beer, pointed at the book.

'You still treating books like shit, I see,' he said. 'I remember you once ripped the cover of one of my books to make a roach for a joint.'

'I never did that,' I said. 'You accused me of that, but it was never proven.'

'Oh, I know it was you,' Rish said. 'I know it and you know it too.'

'What book was it, anyway?'

'I don't know,' he said. 'I don't read any more. Can't seem to concentrate.'

From here: a million conversations. Books to get him out of the slump. Books I'd read. Books I loved and books he'd once loved. Bookshops that had opened. Bookshops that had closed. And music too. What are you listening to these days? A million conversations, but no. No.

'Do you know what Kelly's Eye means?' I asked.

'Like in bingo?' Rish said.

'Yes.'

'Something to do with Ned Kelly?'

'I'm impressed,' I said.

'A guess, that's all,' he said and he smiled.

'And,' I said, not able to stop myself. 'Did you know James Mason was born in Huddersfield?'

'Really?' he said. 'That's funny.'

He laughed and he said he was going to use the toilet.

*

The Chequers, Walthamstow, a pint of Five Points Pale, a solo drink, bags full of shopping from the supermarket and a battered book open on the table, four pints and they know I like my beer in a straight glass, not a jug, and there's WiFi for work emails and personal emails and a text from a friend who's in town and looking for people to drink with and in the process of declining the invite an unknown number on the phone and perhaps it's an opportunity to claw back mis-sold PPI, but instead the slight pause and then his breath, his voice ragged, like shouting at the television during a football match, and his voice saying she's gone, left and gone for good this time, no chance, no chance now, and I am coming home now, flights booked and there is no chance no and there is nothing left and I need to talk to you, and only you, I need you, Noah, and you are the only person, Noah, the only one, and it will be better, it will be better the two of us together like it was, the two of us together.

*

There was only the old soldier. Nothing left to say, except to ask Rish what he thought about a man he'd never even seen. I watched Rish descend the staircase. I realized I could not even describe the army man. His fatigues, yes, but not how he looked. Just a few signs of his age. Enough to ask the question about him. Rish was at the foot of the staircase. There were twenty-seven beers on draught.

I looked down. I was sending a text message or email, not waiting. Not ever. Not waiting at all. I smiled. He sat down. He took a sip of his drink and he had water blooms on the cuff of his jacket.

'Before,' I said. 'There was a man sitting over the other side of the bar. He was wearing full battle fatigues. Desert warfare – sand coloured and all that. But he looked too old to be army. How old can you be as a soldier?'

He shrugged and looked out of the window.

'I read somewhere once that most soldiers don't ever kill anyone,' he said. 'That when confronted with the idea of killing another human being they simply can't do it. There's a sort of switch that just stops them from functioning. From finishing the job. It's like there's a basic humanity, a kind of hard-wired notion of preserving the species.'

The question hung, but neither of us asked it. There was a conversation there. Something to say. A long, involved conversation. One that mattered. One of us just needed to ask: do you think you could? Do you think you could kill someone? Who would you kill? We didn't ask. Neither of us. Another time, this would have been the whole afternoon.

Rish is my oldest, closest friend. The Tap has twenty-seven beers on draught and only one toilet. Rish is the only man I trust with my life. The toilet is upstairs, too; at the top of a spiral staircase, steep and narrow. Rish is the person I love most in the world. You wouldn't have thought it would be allowed, what with Health & Safety. Rish understands me better than I understand myself. The bingo call Kelly's Eye references the famous fugitive Ned Kelly. Rish called me first when it happened. There was a man in here in battle fatigues. Rish had a child he named after me. James Mason was born in Huddersfield. Rish has seen things that I will never see, and has felt things that I can never share.

Outside a delivery from the Camden Hells brewery was in progress. Rish watched it. I watched it too.

'This place has twenty-seven beers on draught,' Rish said, his eyes on the kegs and casks rolling down into the cellar. 'But only one toilet.'

'The toilet's upstairs too,' I said. 'Up those narrow stairs.'

'I'm amazed it's allowed,' Rish said. 'What with Health & Safety and all.'

'How was your flight?' I asked.

'Don't fly American,' he said. 'Never fly American. Seriously. The stewards are the most miserable bastards. And the movies are shit. Never again.'

The Tap has twenty-seven beers on draught. Twenty-seven beers on draught and only one toilet. This is something to say.

Yes.

SUNDOWNERS

He is still talking. She sits, wrapped in a green towel, underwear in her right hand. She catches part of a sentence – 'And this is what people don't understand; you're right, Evelyn, it's exactly as you said . . .' – but Ross does not explain what Evie has said, or he has already explained it and she has not heard, and she smiles though he is not exactly looking at her. On the dressing table is her hairbrush, wooden-handled, a present from her husband.

Evie brushes out her hair, caramelized at the root, pale ale at the tip. She brushes out her hair and wrinkles her feet. The carpeting is thin and she can feel the boards beneath. There is dust on the mirror, a fine sheen, not quite enough to sign her name.

He doesn't wash the towels. He has never washed the towels, this she has recently realized.

'. . . bastards just don't get it—'

'Ross?' she says.

'. . . it's all coming down and they're all just—'

'Ross?' she says. 'Please can you please just *stop*?'

He looks away from whatever imagined audience he's been addressing and turns to her; he pushes his spectacles up the bridge of his nose, a tic to pause time.

'Are you okay?' he asks.

He wears his struck-dumb face, his how-have-I-offended-you? face, his this-is-the-face-of-a-penitent face. Such a sensitive flower. Such a stupid, clever boy. Once, early on, she told him she could listen to him talk all day and all night. That he had liked.

'You really need to clean this place,' she says. 'Wash your towels. And your sheets. Everything really.'

'What?' he says. The springs of the long-rented bed twang as he stands. He looks around. The open wardrobe, the broken lamp on the bedside table: the view as imagined by an impartial observer.

'It's not so bad,' he says, his hand leaning against the window sill. 'It's just cosmetic is all.'

'I'm not arguing with you,' she says. 'Clean this place up or I'm not coming back.'

She gives her hair one last violent brush and Ross nervously laughs. His curls bounce; his white teeth visible, framed by a scrub of beard.

'I mean it.' When she says this, she hears her mother-voice.

'It's never bothered you before,' he says. The spread of

dark hair across his chest converges in a line down to his penis. His nipples are tiny, like a boy's.

He walks over to her and puts his hands on her shoulders, rubs up and down her arms, crouches to meet her eyes.

'Okay,' he says. 'I'll clean up.'

She knows he will lean his forehead against hers. This is when he asks her, always now.

'Don't,' she says. 'Don't ask me. I don't know. I'll call you when I can.'

'Will I need to provide evidence that I've cleaned?' His smile is tentative and is left unmet.

'I'll just walk straight out again if it's like this,' she says.

He moves his hands up from her hips, attempts to unfurl the knot of her towel.

'And don't start that now,' she says. 'I need to get to the shops before they close.' The mother-voice again.

Evie's kiss is swiftly finished and kills any hope Ross might have that she'll throw the towel to the floor. He watches her walk across the landing to the bathroom and as she feels him watching, her gait slows. She looks back over her shoulder, flashes a pin-up girl smile and closes the door.

In the small bathroom two condoms are draped over the lip of the wash-hand basin. She throws them into the small bin and washes herself. The room smells of urine deep in the carpet pile, toothpaste, lemon zest from the soap. Her jeans and blouse are folded on the toilet seat. She pulls them on quickly. Ross walks past the bathroom door; she can hear the hem of his jeans scuffing the cheap carpet. She waits and hears the soft thump of music in the next room. She ties back her hair, picks up her small bottle of perfume and unlocks the door.

Ross is sitting on the corduroy sofa, drinking the wine she spurned on arrival, his jeans low on his hips. Wood-chip walls, books on brick-and-plank shelves, papers spread across a glass coffee table, a portable television, a record player.

'I hate you leaving,' he says as she applies perfume. 'I wish you could stay for ever.'

'No you don't,' she says. 'You'd like to think that, but you don't.'

He stands. He is not as tall as her husband, but fills space more effectively. Even in an empty room he could never be coy.

'Sometimes you scare me, Evelyn,' he says. 'You know that?'

But she just smiles – *you cheeky boy* – as she picks up her handbag from the armchair and checks for her purse and car keys. He drinks his wine. He is the only man she knows who drinks wine.

She points at the glass. 'You keep on like that and you'll get flabby,' she says. 'The women won't flock to you then. When you're fat and flabby.'

Know a lover's weak spots better even than their erogenous zones – a tip from a magazine. As a child and youth, Ross had been an improbable kind of fat – *like a body inflated with sausage meat*: his own description. Everyone called him Chip Shop. Not everyone, he realized even as he told her this, but enough to make it feel so. They said he smelled of the deep-fat fryers his father owned and operated. They said he smelled of fish. It was, he told her, better than being called Yid.

'I only drink when I'm with you,' he says. For a man proud of his acumen, he says things like this too often.

'Well it's best I leave now, then. Before you turn fat and unlovable.'

He shakes his head and drains the glass.

'Must you do this every time?' he says.

'Do what?'

'You know . . . this,' he says windmilling his arms, the tiny red heart in the wineglass jumping. 'This . . . decompressing.'

'What does that even mean?' she says.

'You know exactly what it means,' he says. Evie moves towards him, leans in, kisses him, holds her right hand to his left cheek.

'You credit me with far too much intent, Ross. It's endearing.'

He kisses her in a violent manner he is only now learning to enjoy.

'I'll call you,' she says. 'I don't know when. But I will.'

'I'm supposed to be waiting?' he says. 'For more of the same?'

'If you have the time, yes,' she says.

'Time's running out, I keep telling you this,' he says.

'I know,' she says, walking to the door. 'The bombs could drop at any time.'

*

Evie closes Ross's front door in soft afternoon light and follows the row of doors – all the same shade of blue, some with pot-plants outside, some with children's bicycles tethered to nearby drainpipes – towards the stairwell. The road and cars below are sun-lit, but the walkway remains in shade. She holds her breath against the piss smell as she descends.

On the street all is quiet. The newly built flats opposite are a grid of windows, six by six. In three across, two up, a woman stands, her body framed by purple curtains. Evie sees her most times she visits – how quaint to call it a visit! – and had once waved to her. The woman had not waved back, but disappeared quickly into darkness. She does the same now, sees Evie and, holding her cup of tea and saucer, darts back into the gloom. Evie can imagine the woman sitting on a plump-cushioned armchair, biscuits arranged on a plate, telling the policeman – so young, so short these days – that she'd seen the woman many times. Yes: many times. She looked the sort, you know.

Evie's car – rusting, a small red Ford with just enough room for the four of them – is parked next to a dirty-panelled white van. Kids have used their fingers to write obscenities on it, jokes on it, DS 4 RB on it. Phil and Chris will soon be old enough to do the same: leave a mark, show off to their friends, or a girl. Their fingers, their only current offence being to pick at their noses, might soon write fuck or cunt anywhere.

Evie sits in the car with the key in the ignition. She doesn't like to drive away immediately; she enjoys the airport feeling of concurrence: the wish to stay, the wish to return home. The car is hot and her thighs would stick to the leatherette seat if she was wearing a skirt. When Jim used to pick her up in his car, his borrowed car, her then-narrower thighs did that; made a sucking sound too when she got out of the passenger side. Somewhere in the loft those skirts are bundled and folded inside a packing case. She reminds herself to hunt them out, but her attention is diverted by something sticking out from under the passenger seat. She leans over and with her fingertips teases out some brightly coloured paper. When she straightens it, she's holding the wrapper from a chocolate bar.

Evie does not eat chocolate bars. She holds the wrapper, holds it like it could be infected, and wonders whether it could somehow incriminate her: whether it could have covert meaning to someone else.

No, she could not have left it there. Nor Ross; he has never been inside her car. It is just a Mars Bar wrapper. *Advertising and branding as distraction. Ever more sophisticated stratagems to ensure we are good consumers. Work, Rest and Pay.* Talking, talking the way he does, impatient. She admires and is amused by his seriousness. Everything is important. The world is connected and running towards its end. *Can you please just stop?*

'Come on,' she says. 'The kettle's boiling.'

She blows the wrapper from her palm and it floats down to the rubber mat on the passenger side.

Waiting for the kettle to boil while the world burns crazy. Another Ross phrase. At functions, coffee mornings, schoolyard gates, she finds herself thinking *the kettle's boiling* as she smiles and listens to people talking at her. Sometimes she says it out loud and people look at her blankly. She ducks her head then, pours more tea or buttons up her cardigan. No one has ever asked her what she means.

'Come on,' she says again. The key remains unturned in the ignition, the car still sticky hot. She looks at her watch but there's plenty of time to pick up the boys. She turns the key and turns on the radio. But the radio is broken, it just plays static, and she tells herself to remind Jim to mend it. On the passenger side, on the rubber mat, the chocolate bar wrapper lies. She picks it up and stuffs it in her handbag. We are all detectives.

She starts the car and pulls into the road. The car has had no other passengers, which means either the boys or Jim must have eaten it. The boys are not allowed sweets during the week, even during the school holidays. So it has to be Jim's chocolate bar. She is uncomfortable with this deduction.

In all the years she has known Jim, all the intimacies they have shared, she has never seen him eat a bar of chocolate. Does he even like chocolate? She brakes at a red light. Does he even eat chocolate cake?

How can I not be sure of this? Stopped at a box junction, she tries to remember him eating cake, not as part of any ritual, no wedding or birthday cakes, but just cake: at people's houses, at coffee mornings, at her mother's home years ago. She cannot recall a single chocolate cake amongst them.

Evie turns onto the A-road. To her right and left there are fields and hills and Friesian cows. She lists Jim's favourite food: medium-rare steak and chips; liver, onions and bacon; roast lamb on a Sunday. Food that he chooses when there is a choice – birthdays, anniversaries. The dishes only he cooks: cawl, corned-beef hash, toad in the hole. Tonight is rabbit-food night, salad and the last of the beef, sliced thinly. There is beetroot? There is beetroot. Tomatoes looked a little tired this morning, but cut up chunky will be fine. A chocolate bar. Just one. It has to be him. Enough salad cream? There is for tonight.

There are five separate almost-incidents on the way home but they amount to nothing: she misses other vehicles or they miss her. At the roundabout, a man sounds his horn as she undercuts him. She sees him dumbshowed behind the driver's side window; an angry reddened face shouting. Evie keeps her eyes on the road, vigilant and chastened. *Stupid girl.* Her mother's voice. She turns onto Buglawton Street and approaches St Mark's Church.

The other parents, mothers all, are already gathered at the churchyard railings. Evie pulls in by the corner shop and gets out of the car, throws the Mars Bar wrapper into a yellow litter bin bracketed to a streetlamp. *Keep Britain Tidy.* She spots Deborah to the right of a yew tree and waves. Evie can hear the kids singing in the church hall as she crosses the road, a chorus of plaintive voices over a pounding upright piano. It takes her a while to make out the tune, the *Match of the Day* song again. The lyrics *I want to live my life with Jesus / and walk his narrow way* fitting surprisingly well. The boys have been singing it at home, singing it as they kick a ball to each other, as they dribble past each other, singing it even as the game ends in the inevitable scrap and tangle.

'My Stephen won't stop singing that bloody song,' Deborah says under the flopping brim of a sun hat.

'My two are the same,' Evie says. 'They don't know what it means though. Not a clue as far as I can tell.'

'The vicar must despair.'

Deborah is freckled and sun-blushed; fine auburn hair, thin body and perfect pregnant bump. The two could be sisters, though Evie has her Gallic nose. Deborah's second child is asleep in a pushchair, the same model Jim gave away to a neighbour. No: not the same model, she sees looking at it again; older, actually, bigger wheels.

'How've you been?' Evie says. 'Must be hard now it's warm.'

'I get hot at night, but it's not so bad. Better than the last one anyway. Alan bought me one of those electric fans and that's lovely. Like being on holiday.'

The kids reach the end of the song – they can't call it a hymn, it's too much fun – and the parents hear the young vicar ask for quiet and calm before prayers. All the kids know when to say Amen and all the words to the Lord's Prayer, though Chris and Phil have been arguing over exactly what constitutes daily bread: does it include the crusty loaf Jim buys only on Saturdays?

'How is Alan?' Evie asks. Deborah's husband Alan has a tool for every job and a ready smile: the brand of man her father admired, the brand of man Ross says will be swatted by technology. Computers will come and destroy these men, he has said, and we will not mourn them as we should. When it comes, they will inherit the earth. As Ross said this, she'd laughed.

'What's funny about that,' he'd said. 'Don't you understand what I'm saying?'

'That we're quite useless. That books will count for nothing if there's nothing to eat, no shelter, no power. That chopping wood is—'

'You're mocking me,' he said.

'Yes,' she said. 'Someone has to.'

Evie looks down to the baby in the pushchair.

'He's fine. Jim?' Deborah says.

'Fine,' Evie says and smiles at the little girl, Deidra. Huge eyes and eyelashes, thick fronds below auburn eyebrows. Crusted snot on the nose, odd numbered teeth: perfect. The cheek skin is cool, the hair thin and priceless. Evie momentarily remembers herself taking

Ross's circumcised penis in her mouth. His beard against her thighs. Sees him walk to the bathroom removing a condom. Evie is relieved to hear an emphatic Amen at the end of the Lord's Prayer.

The kids flood through the graveyard, behind them the young vicar and his volunteers. Some of them are holding drawings, oversized pieces of sugar paper. Evie scans the small crowd and can't see Phil or Chris. They are not there. They have been taken. She darts her head left and right. The boys are not there. They are under the mud and turf of the moors. She'll have to explain where she's been. That earlier today she was fucking a man five years her junior in a rented flat a few miles over the county border. That she has done so almost every day of the summer holidays. Then Chris and Phil are there, kicking a tennis ball between them, Deborah's Stephen bringing up the rear.

Evie's boys are sandy haired and, despite the heat, both wearing their football scarves. Phil has a cold that won't shift and sniffs constantly because he won't blow his nose. Little Flip. Little Sniff. They do not have drawings; they never do. They look up and wave at their mother, run towards her.

'I scored five goals,' Chris says.

'I scored three,' Phil says.

'Well done,' she says. 'But do you have to wear those scarves? You must be boiling.'

She tries to take them from their necks, but the boys wriggle away. She has done the same every afternoon since they started coming here.

'See you tomorrow, Evie,' Deborah says.

Evie nods and leads the boys to the car. Moments like this – watching Little Flip open the car door; hearing Chris buckle his seatbelt, smelling the stink from one of their behinds – come to her when Ross talks of a *confetti* of bombs, of a total *solar occlusion*.

'The thing is, Ross,' she'd said, interrupting him the first time, naked and dangling a wine glass between her fingers. 'The thing is that the end of the world's just a young man's worry.'

Ross shook his head and started to say something. She cut him off, delightedly.

'Don't shake your head' – a mother – 'look at you. Young, healthy, good breeding, good prospects. To you, the bomb is the only visible threat. It's the only *viable* threat. You talk about blast radiuses and fallout and nuclear winters, and to you it sounds plausible. But to me . . .' – she laughed – 'the end of the world is a drunk driver, a kidnapper, whooping cough, leukaemia, meningitis, cot death, railway electrocution, fireworks, a fall from a tree . . .'

Sunlight eased through the curtains' gap, a certain decadence to its fall. The two of them shared a silence as heavy as the fabric keeping out the afternoon. She rarely mentioned the boys, even obliquely. Now, towards the end of the summer, when he talks about her and him, he sometimes mentions them and for Evie the illusion, so playfully curated, splinters like a dropped glass.

That afternoon, she watched his penis slowly retreat until snug against his scrotum.

'What about Cuba?' he said, leaning over and picking up the packet of cigarettes.

'What about Cuba?' she said and moved onto her side, her head supported by her palm.

The match flared, smoke pooled, was sucked in with a pop, was exhaled in two bold lines through his nose.

'You hid in your room,' he said sitting yogi-like, staring at her. He drew on the cigarette. 'You made a shelter.' The last syllable was smoky; she waved it away.

'No,' she said. 'No I didn't.'

'That's what you told me.'

He looked mischievous; all she felt was exhaustion. *I could listen to you all day and all night.*

'No. I said Ada and I didn't leave the house that whole week. I didn't say anything about a shelter.'

Ada with the gin and the cigarettes; the aftermath of the abortion. The transistor radio and cold-eaten soup. Come on the fucking bombs. Ada at the window: Drop them now! Let's see the whites of their eyes! Come, hail them down on us!

'You cocooned yourself. You and your best friend. You were afraid and you cocooned yourself. I'm interested: are you saying this was somehow childish? Now you have children you can see the error of your ways? Do I have your argument right?'

'That's not what I meant,' she said. 'Not at all. We *used* the missile crisis. It was convenient. It was dramatic. Has there ever been a greater drama? A greater collective breath? And all we were talking about was a boy who'd run off because Ada got *in the family way*. Those were the words we used. That was what we were talking about. I don't think we talked about Khrushchev or Kennedy. Ada was so drunk she wouldn't have been able to pronounce their names. But when you have children—'

'I told you, I could never bring children into this world,' he said and looked down to his groin. 'I've always said that.'

'So you have. Okay, when you grow up, then,' she said, her slow laugh throaty. 'When you grow up, you'll forget about three-minute warnings. The apocalypse will feel like a ghost story. One of those late-night campsite fables.'

He stubbed out his cigarette. He looked pityingly at her; how little she knew. She watched him and wanted to shake him. Tell him that his certainty was both infuriating and unwarranted.

'That morning,' he said eventually, 'that first morning, they took us to the gym after morning prayers,' he said, looking away from Evie and over to the window. 'And gave us the instructions. Duck and cover, you remember, right? It was the first time I noticed the teachers were afraid too. Young and afraid. And so we make our way back from the gym and soon it's all over the sixth form. Joy Andrews has set up a raffle. All those without a boyfriend or girlfriend, which was most of us, would be entered. Everyone should have someone to love at the end of the world, she said. She bought raffle tickets and each girl was given a number, the boys left to draw their partner for the last day of being alive. I'd been in love with Ruth Calendar for two years and her number was twenty-three. The things you remember!'

He roughed his hand through his hair.

'Joy came to me in the science block and handed me the straw hat. I put my hand in and visualized twenty-three. I searched it out and opened the piece of paper. She'd folded it five, six times. It said twenty-two. I couldn't believe it. So close! Joy smiled and told me that my wife for the end of the world was Alice Bergman. Alice fucking Bergman.

'She was as fat as me, fatter even. I saw her across the

playground and the look between us was about as close to hatred as I've ever known. But it was inevitable: the two fatties together. I could have picked a billion times and it would always have been her. Alice fucking Bergman.'

He expected Evie to be looking at him, but her eyes were on the window, on the curtains.

'Who would you fuck now if the bombs were coming?' he said. 'Your last fuck on earth.'

She sat up.

'What kind of a question is that?' she said.

'A straight one.' He shifted up in the bed.

'That's a straight question?'

A sudden gust blew the curtains, bright-lit the room, then dimmed.

'Yes,' he said. 'No.' He smiled and kissed her.

'Ignore me,' he said. 'I don't know what I'm talking about.'

'No,' she said. 'No you don't.'

*

Holding a mug of tea, Evie opens the back door and sits on one of the two folding chairs set out on the flagged side-return. She blows on the tea and watches her two boys taking it in turns to fire the football at the makeshift goal. Despite their round little faces and bowl haircuts, they swear like navvies when they think she's not around.

Both she and Jim find their children's accents strange. You wait for your children to talk, but there's no control over how their words will sound. Voiceprints are unique, like dabs. She feels sure she would be able to pick their voices out from a line up. She sips her tea and listens to them, their tongues unguarded now, both believing she's inside.

'. . . You dick . . .'

'. . . Fuck off, dick . . .'

'. . . Fucking dick . . .'

'. . . No, you fucking dick . . .'

'. . . Fucking dickhead . . .'

She's still smiling as she closes the door. The clock on the wall says one minute after six and she watches the second hand, red and thin, stutter round the face. She guesses it will be seven minutes past when the front door opens, when Jim's arms are around her, when he asks her what she's done with her day. Time for a sundowner? he'll say. And they'll share first a kiss, and then a bottle of beer before dinner.

*

In the small kitchen she begins to prepare the plates of salad. The boys will complain, so she puts on potatoes for mash. The radio news is all about the latest in Northern Ireland. The violence is more distant in her kitchen; at

Ross's he beckons it into the room. He admires the struggle, admires any kind of struggle, even though they are all doomed, all fucked, he says.

Jim takes the beef joint from the fridge and begins to sharpen the carving knife. She looks out the window to the small garden. There is only a finite number of musical notes, yet we have not run out of music. Conversation is the same. There is always something to say, always something to fill the silence. We will fill the world with things, Ross says, just so we can talk about them. Clever boy.

'We're hungry,' the boys say.

'That's funny, we're Poland,' Jim used to reply. He doesn't any longer.

'Tea'll be ready in ten minutes,' Evie says. 'Can you lay the table?'

They take the placemats from the sideboard and throw them down. She passes them knives and forks, mustard and salad cream. Jim slices the beef thinly and adds it to the salad. She checks on the potatoes, drains them and begins to mash.

'Did you . . .' she says as she watches the white mush smooth through the holes of the masher. 'Did you have a Mars Bar the other day?'

He takes a chunk of cucumber and pops it in his mouth, his face as guilty as an apple scrumper's.

'A Mars Bar?'

'Yep, you know, work rest and play.'

'No, no, I don't think so. I don't remember having one.'

'There was a wrapper in the car this afternoon.'

She doesn't look up at him, but down at the mash, trying to get out all the lumps.

'Actually, yes. I remember now. I had one the other morning. I felt a bit light-headed, so I bought one at the newsagent's. Why do you ask?'

Evie hooks a shank of hair behind her ear, her face pink from the exertion of mashing.

'I couldn't remember you ever eating one that's all.'

'When I was a child a friend of my dad's gave me some chocolate-covered Turkish delight and I was sick all night. But I was in the newsagent's and I thought the sugar would do me good.'

Evie looks at him as she spoons mash onto the plates. When she is full she cannot imagine ever eating again, cannot bear the sight of other people tucking into big dinners. No, not Jim. Never Jim.

The boys leave most of their salad and the usual bargaining ensues. They are good kids; she says this to herself and means it, but teatime is trying. She lets Jim be the bad guy this time, as cucumber and beetroot are counted into mouths, quarters of boiled egg passed between plates. Eventually she calls time and they are allowed to choose

a yoghurt each from the fridge. Jim stacks the plates and
puts them by the sink.

'Who'd like a walk after dinner?' Jim says. 'We could
go up to Bluebell Wood.'

'*Dad*,' Chris says.

'Will you go in goal for us when we get back?' Phil
says. Little Flip.

'We'll see,' he says. Always, we'll see.

'Just for half an hour?' Chris says.

'We'll see.'

The small back garden looks out over a series of
fields leading to a farm at the crest of a hill. They duck
under the barbed wire at the back of the garden and
walk along the path beside their neighbours' houses. The
boys kick the football *Keegan/Toshack/Keegan/Toshack*
as they pass it between them. Sun fades over the hill.
Evie holds Jim's hand as they walk, having slipped it into
his when offered. We are all detectives.

Jim stops by the stile on the way into Bluebell Wood.
The boys are running ahead, hoofing the ball high into the
air and trying to head it on its descent.

'In the paper today,' Jim says. 'There was an interview
with a woman who should have been on that plane that
crashed in June. You remember? She's been in hospital for
months, can't cope with it, mentally I mean. She saw the

plane come down, she said. Before the flight. She saw it and refused to get on. Imagine that.'

'Amazing,' she says, looking up ahead to the boys.

'People who see things,' he says. 'Get premonitions. You never hear about those that got it wrong, do you? Only those that got it right. Every time there's a plane crash there's always someone who "saw" it, who got the feeling the plane would go down.' He steps down the stile. 'And cancelled their ticket. How many people do that a day, I wonder? How many seats go empty because some passenger has a *feeling*?'

'I can't imagine.'

'It can't be insignificant.'

'Someone I met once was convinced there'd be a nuclear war by 1980,' she says. Ross. After the CND March, around a small table in a Manchester pub, after the biting March cold, and him leaning into her saying: 'I would like to see you again. Soon. There is no time to be wasted.'

Jim stops.

'Just because a button's there doesn't mean it'll be pressed.'

'He thought the opposite.'

Jim shakes his head.

'Well, I feel sorry for him, then. To live every day as if it could end before sun-up or sun-down. Imagine that.'

He smiles at that. She puts her hand in the back pocket of his jeans.

The bluebells were startling in the late spring, but now are dead-headed and a drained shade of purple. There is a rope swing over a small gulch that the boys have been scared off using with a cautionary tale about the kid who is now pushed around town in a wheelchair. They walk along the narrow pathway; there are cigarette ends and cans of beer and she hopes they will not stumble upon a condom.

She'd asked Ross to leave it off just once. He had refused. It would be wrong, he said, even to countenance the creation of a new life in this dying world. All she wanted, she said, was to feel him inside her properly, just once; was that so wrong?

Evie still has her hand in Jim's back pocket. Chris is holding the football and Little Flip is trying to get at it.

'Stop that,' Jim says. 'And watch out for stinging nettles.'

They circle the wood and the gulch stinks, spindly creatures on its scummy top, the rope swing idling in the breeze. Jim leans down to kiss her neck. He will want sex tonight. The thought is not unpleasant.

When she dreams of her unborn child, which is too often and not enough, she is sometimes able to take the dream in hand and keep it reeling. It is precarious, but she can hold the baby for longer, concentrating on her as the fantasy fades. She is then awake and alone. She goes to the bathroom to piss and knows that the seat will be down because Jim understands that this is one of those things. Good boy, he is.

*

Philip and Chris are in bed and the front room is messy with toys. She puts them in the big wooden box Jim made. He is in the kitchen, the kettle whistling, the paper spread out on the table open at the crossword. He puts two cups of tea next to the paper and sits down. She sits beside him and takes in the half-complete crossword. He reads out clues he has not yet solved. She always holds out a faint hope that a clue might be repeated, that he will read it out and she will be able to say 'we've had this one before', but the clues are always new and always unguessable. Perhaps Ross is wrong about technology defeating boredom: Jim is never bored by the crossword.

The phone rings as they fill out the penultimate clue. The sound is still a surprise. Neither of them saw the point, save for emergencies, and there's a phone box at the end of the road. But in the end, they got one anyway.

'What the devil?' Jim says. What he always says when it rings.

'I'll get it,' Evie says and goes into the hallway. She

picks up the receiver and answers with a curt hello. Jim always reels off their telephone number, posed as a question. There is silence on the other end of the line and then pips.

'Evelyn, I need to see you,' Ross says. 'It's important.'

'Oh, hello, love,' she says. 'Kids down, are they?'

'Tonight,' he says. 'Meet me tonight?'

'No, no,' she says. 'Mine are down. Though the little horrors are probably reading comics by torchlight.'

'I'm not fucking about, Evelyn. I need to see you. I need to see you tonight.'

'No, I'm not sure I can do that; we're off to bed soon.'

'I wouldn't ask if it wasn't of the utmost importance.'

'Well, I'll talk to Jim and see what he says. Can't promise anything, though.'

'Meet me at the Swettenham Arms at nine.'

'Well, I'll ask and I'll see what I can do.'

The phone goes dead. She replaces the receiver and smears her thumb across its top as though removing fingerprints. She goes to the bathroom and locks the door, sits down on the closed toilet seat.

The weakness, the self-delusion of men. She has been fortunate, though. He has been a distraction and nothing more, the kind of affair that you read about in magazines at the hair salon. Over now. Before anything goes awry.

She flushes the toilet and eyes the telephone as she passes, daring it to ring again.

Jim is writing letters in a circle, trying to unpick an anagram. He looks up and she sees the man she loved and the man she loves. He takes off his spectacles.

'Was that Kath?' he asks.

She sits down at the table and picks up her tea, blows on it.

'She wants me to meet her at the Swettenham Arms. Another crisis, I suspect.'

He kneads his eyes, looks at his watch.

'It's coming up to nine o'clock,' he says. 'Can't she wait until tomorrow?'

'It'll only be for an hour or so.'

'That woman lives in perpetual crisis. She's like the Middle East. Like the bloody Lebanon.'

'I know,' she says. 'But you know what Jeff's like.'

'You go,' he says, his eyes back on the wheel of letters. 'Counsel your flock.'

She kisses him on the top of his head and he looks up and smiles. She thinks of the Mars Bar again. Him eating it on the way out of the newsagent's.

'Do you often get light-headed?' she says.

'What?' he says.

'You said you got light-headed and that's why you had that Mars Bar. I just wondered if it happens a lot.'

'Not really,' he says. 'Sometimes, but it happens to everyone, doesn't it? It was nothing, just leaving the house without breakfast, that's all.'

'I've told you I don't mind making—'

'I know, but I can sort my own breakfast out. I'm not a hopeless case, you know?'

'I know that, love. But still—'

'I'm fine, okay?' he says. 'It was just the once.'

'Yes,' she says. 'I just worry, that's all.'

'Go and worry about Kath,' he says.

She kisses him.

'See you in bed,' he says.

*

In the car she pauses with the key in the ignition. She never wanted an affair; she only wanted a lover. The way the French do it; the gentility of a marriage with an outlet for unspent passion. But there is nothing French about this, nothing elegant.

She pulls out of the driveway and takes a left at the end of the road. She realizes she hasn't said goodbye to the boys. She almost turns back.

'Do not die,' she says. 'Do not have an accident.'

The Swettenham Arms is a grotto; a thatched roof and wattle and daub. It looks inviting, like a coach house from an old book. The kettle's boiling, she says, as she parks the car.

He is sitting in the snug, a glass of beer in front of him. Evie goes to the bar and orders a gin and tonic. She sits down at the small table. He is smoking and she is smiling, dumbly.

'I told you never, under any circumstances, to call the house,' she says, still smiling.

'I needed to see you,' he says. He is not looking at her but down at the ashtray.

'I must be mad,' she says.

'There is only madness,' he says, finally looking up. The beard and the eyes; the curl of smoke. 'That's all there is.'

'You're drunk, aren't you? Drunk and bloody stupid.'

He takes a sip of his drink then takes her hand. She pulls it away.

'You risk everything for me,' he says. 'Everything. And all I do is talk. I talk and talk and you listen and nothing changes. I've been thinking about it since you left. Nothing else. And it can't wait, not another moment.'

Ross tries to put his hands on hers again and again she quickly moves hers away. She wonders whether something has unhinged him; whether he has always been unhinged. *Idiot.* She says it out loud and he looks at her, laughs and shakes his head.

'Yes,' he says. 'Yes.'

He looks at her fixedly now. 'Listen,' he says. 'Listen.'

He stubs out his cigarette, rubs his hand across his mouth.

'I want you to leave Jim,' he says. 'I want you to leave Jim with the boys and come and live with me.'

She laughs; head angled back, exaggerated.

'I want to have a child with you,' he says quietly. 'Our own child. Just ours.'

She has a taste like aspirin in the back of her throat. He is holding her hands suddenly, and she does not pull hers back, not straight away. Such blue eyes, such a scrabbly beard. How beautiful a girl would be with his eyelashes. The air is warm and muggy. Somewhere there are bombs.

Ross as father. Drunk drivers, a kidnapping, whooping cough, leukaemia, meningitis, cot death, railway electrocution, fireworks, a fall from a tree.

'I mean it,' Ross says. 'I mean every word.'

She pauses before standing up.

'It's time to go,' she says.

'No,' he says. 'No it isn't.'

She doesn't say anything. She gets up and leaves and does not look back. She does not want to see the baby in his arms; she does not want to see her blonde hair. She does not want to see her mouth calling mama.

Outside, her car and his. Side by side. She gets inside

hers, puts the key in the ignition. Later he will do the same.

There will be no accident on the way home. They will neither die nor be injured, lose a limb or eye. They will no longer talk of bombs or unborn children. They will, the two of them, disappear into family life, wander into it, fall into it, fade slowly into it. They will, the two of them, never be seen again.

YOUR FATHER SENDS HIS LOVE

1

He can remember everything. A whole life, all of it. Every moment, every detail; every breath, every beat. Everything, all the way back to the moment of his birth. Sitting in the annexe, under lamplight, of this he is momentarily certain. Certain he can relive every last second; certain he can live his life over. A whole life in a straight line from birth to death; from childhood to old age. No digressions. No jokes. No anecdotes. Just truth following truth, fact following fact. How simple, how easy it seems, sitting in the annexe, under the lamplight. How simple and clear.

A video recorder begins to pull and wind; another stops spooling. There are three more in the annexe, all silent, all programmed. He looks down at the rug, up at the blank television screen. He does not remember everything. He cannot remember everything; the very idea is ridiculous. He cannot recall the moment of his birth any more than he can his first breath. He cannot even remember his mother's face.

Instead of breath and cry, he recalls a line in one of his notebooks. Second volume, fifth page, sixteenth section. He wrote it in a hotel room in Great Yarmouth: shabby dresser, wrinkled sheets. *This is a true story; I know, I made it up myself.* It was written in pencil, the only thing he had to hand, beneath a series of jokes about Red Indians and above the outline for a barbershop routine.

He can remember everything in the notebooks. Every joke, every idea; every sketch, every pun. He knows this is true. Turn seven pages and the third line is in blue ink, written while on a flight to Barbados. *I came home to find my son taking drugs – all my best ones, too.*

The two books are locked in the wall safe. They once had their own bag, once toured and travelled along with Bob. They no longer leave the annexe. They were once stolen. His whole life, from first to last. When they stole them, they took everything from him. He still says that. He still says they stole the books. They stole his life. They.

*

In London, in its white heat and cold winters, four dead sons. Four stillbirths, four long silences, four coffinless mournings. He remembers the taxi rides, but not the hospitals. The taxi rides.

One in winter: the taking off and on of gloves, the wrapping of scarves, the look on his wife's face, on her raided face. Do not speak. Do not make light. Do not joke.

One in summer: the cabbie picking him up alone, back to the Golders Green house. The cabbie's feminine eyelashes, his vinegary body odour. A joke told and Bob's laugh. Bob's second dead son and him laughing.

'You can have that one for free,' the cabbie said.

'You'll never make it as a cabbie if you give passengers tips,' Bob said and the cabbie laughed and Bob laughed. Bob caught his own reflection in the rear-view mirror, pale as bone, hair quick-laced with grey.

Another in wind-blown October, alone again. A silent cabbie aside from his metronomic sniffing. Asking the cabbie to stop at the off-licence and buying a bottle of Scotch, looking at the cigars. The single ones in tins, packs of three and five. A moment braced with emotion and then nothing. A packet of Player's, too. Make it two packs of Player's. Outside, the taxi idling, two old Jews walking past. His mother's voice. The way she said *Jew*. If she'd known about the dead boys, she'd have said she'd warned him. She'd warned him but he'd not listened.

What did I say? What did I say at the outset? You never listen. You never learn. You may as well have married a Jew. At least the Jews have all the money. The Irish just have chippy shoulders and thieving hands. No wonder the children keep dying. No wonder there's no son and heir.

*You should . . . a nice girl. A nice English girl. Nice man-
ners. A sherry drinker. Clean limbed and well-spoken.
Robert, dear, I love you, which is why I say—*

Oh that face! The mole with the plucked hairs, her
skin the same pallor as his; her wrinkled, clawing hands.
Her arrival at his wedding, the service she said she would
not attend, dressed – as in a joke – in black. Crown to
toenail in black, a veil too. Such impeccable comic timing.
He wished his was as natural.

The last death in the heart of May's confusion. A different hospital, the same outcome. He left his wife to rest
and took a taxi to a woman's apartment in Maida Vale. He
drank her wine, went to her bed, and afterwards looked
out of her window, looked out over stands of trees and
parkland, not thinking of his wife's fitful sleep, not thinking of his four dead sons. Or thinking of them all. He
cannot now be sure.

Nineteen-fifty-two, and the fifth boy arrived three
months early. So small, so early and so small, three months
prem. But breathing, yes; alive, yes. Incubated, a wriggle
of a boy, sharing the white sheets with a girl more runt-
ish kitten than human child. Bob named her Victoria. A
queen in waiting. His son he named Gary. Nothing so
royal, just a name they both liked. Victoria soon lost her
sight. He prayed for his son to keep his sight. The son was
unblind; a small, almost cruel, mercy.

Days and the specialist called them in, days of watching and waiting, the blind child queen taken to her parents; Gary alone on the white sheet. In the hospital there were no pretty nurses or battle-axe matrons. There was carbolic and bleach, uncomfortable chairs, corridors that ran like slick highways. Bob and his wife held hands as they entered the pipe-smoked room the consultants shared. The specialist was a woman, neat and tidy, twinset and pearls. Best in her field, best anywhere. Sitting behind her desk, uncapping a fountain pen.

The specialist invited them to sit. Bob and his wife held hands over the chair arms. The specialist looked down at the file – thin lips, no make-up, hood-eyes, a wiggish hairdo – then up at them.

'There is no easy way to say this,' she said. 'But the tests are clear and they are irrefutable. Your son has cerebral palsy.'

They must have looked. Looked blank perhaps.

'Gary is a spastic,' she said.

She went on. She told them she was sorry, but Gary would never speak, would never hear, would never walk, would never sit himself at a dinner table. She explained in her measured, careful way the ramifications, but all Bob heard was spastic. Her thin lips moving: spastic. Her bobbing head as she looked to her notes: spastic. The look of professional sympathy as she took off her spectacles:

spastic. She had used the word without affect, without thought, and Bob had never heard it spoken before, and could never now unhear it. Spastic. That boy and the word. That beautiful boy. That heart-breaking boy.

*

The annexe is broadly cruciform, the western end longer than planned, extended to accommodate a series of tall octagonal spinners arranged in two banks, heading down to a small round window. On each wall is a unit, in each unit nine shelves, each shelf the height of a VHS cassette plus a quarter inch. Stacks of tapes, some still in cellophane, on the floor and on the desk. The used tapes are labelled and sorted, dated and shelved. An assistant is employed on Wednesdays and Thursdays. He is to tidy up, to label and sort. Bob is never present. He has seen him only twice since he was hired: a pudgy fellow, beetle-browed, the sort who wishes to solve a joke rather than laugh at it.

Bob pours Scotch and gets up from the sofa, crack in the knees, ache in the neck. He walks to the first spinner. As a collection it is kitsch. Every casing, screwhead and stretch of tape documents something in which only he is interested. A library of himself. Thirty-minute memories. Bob pulls out a tape at random. A drama called *The Flip Side*. In it he plays a DJ, a right-wing DJ, plays him with a fire and zeal and a sense of menace; his best work, some of his best work, taut and polished and the director afterwards saying that he should do more serious work, tread the boards, Pinter, Osborne, those kinds of people. He holds the tape, Maxell 180, more programmes on the tape, but the only one worth considering is *The Flip Side*. There is no other example in the world. It exists only in the memory of those who watched it and, thirty-five years later, are still alive and still recall a television drama that was shown only once. It is a plastic legacy, this junk he has collected.

The last time he'd seen *The Flip Side* was twelve years ago. An old friend disputing that Bob had ever done anything aside from making money presenting game shows.

'*The Flip Side*,' Bob said, '1966, *The Flip Side*. The *Radio Times* called it one of the boldest and most chilling performances they'd ever seen. *The Flip Side*. They said I should go on the stage. They said they'd not seen anything like it. Pinter, Osborne, those kind of people. I won a fucking award for that.'

And Bob made the friend put on his shoes and carry his glass to the annexe and they settled down to watch *The Flip Side*. The tape began. Bob was some twenty years younger. He was using an American accent, shaky but not without skill. Bob watched himself, Bob's eyes only for the screen, only for himself. The friend took the remote control and pressed pause.

'Go on, then,' the friend said. 'Do it. You want to do it, you know you want to.'

Bob looked at himself as a young man; a young man paused on the television screen. He smiled at the friend and stood.

'And do you think, listeners,' he said, 'that this is acceptable? That this is the way we are to raise our children these days? With these kinds of morals? With these kinds of codes? We need to think of the children. We need to protect them, we need to nurture them, not pervert them. Not indulge them with such poison and fallen idols . . .'

Standing, Bob delivered line after line, the accent better, more mature than on the videotape. Bob acted and Bob paced, acted and paced as he had decades before, as though life were contingent on his performance. Behind the revival, Bob's younger face was paused, a telephone to his ear. Before Bob could finish, the younger man disappeared, the video recorder automatically releasing the tape. Bob delivered his last line in front of the blank screen. He paused, then bowed, wiped away the sweat from his brow with a pocket square.

Bob remembers his friend's face: soft and sallow,

framed with tight white hair, tobacco teeth, long nose. The way the friend scratched the stubble of his cheek, put down his glass and gave quiet applause. He remembers that but not asking him to talk to Simon for him.

'Shall I do another?' Bob said, standing up, moving to the spinners. 'Pick one. Pick any tape and give me the first line. First line and I'll do the lot. All the parts, all the lines.'

The friend smiled and shook his head.

'Don't think I can't,' Bob said. 'Don't think I can't, because you know I can.'

*

The boy was light in the hand, his legs pedalling air – *getoffgetoffgetoffgetoffgetoff* – until he was arcing through the air onto the small bed. Simon was crying. Bob slapped him across his eight-year-old face.

'Now you listen, you nasty piece of work,' Bob said. 'Listen to your father and stop your crying.'

He wanted to say: 'Or I shall give you something to cry about.' This was how it had gone with his father. Bob sat down on the bed. The boy was howling, a stuck animal, grunting.

'Now look,' Bob said, calming voice, calming, a hand on the boy's arm, then an arm around him. 'You look at me,' Bob said. 'Shhh and look at me.'

Bob combed back the boy's hair, his unruly natural quiff.

'When your brother was born,' Bob said, 'when your brother was born, he wasn't very well. We didn't know what was wrong with him. The doctors they did their tests. And we waited for the results. The results came back and it was cerebral palsy. They told us to see a specialist. And the specialist, she told us Gary was a spastic. That's what she said. And I'd never heard that word before. Now, Simon, I've been called some bad names in my time, and I'd never heard such a bad word before. And I haven't heard a worse one since. So when I heard you call Gary that, when I heard you use that awful word, I couldn't believe my ears. I couldn't believe my own son would be able to use that word to taunt his own brother. So I want you to apologize to Gary and I want you to swear you'll never use that word again. Not now, not ever. Do you understand?'

Simon nodded.

'And you promise? Promise on your life?'

Simon nodded.

'Because I can send you away if you do. Don't think I can't, because you know I can.'

Simon leaned in to his father and cried as he was held. Bob took him to his brother's room. Bob watched him, red-eyed, say sorry to his brother; kiss his brother on his handsome face. On his handsome cheek. And the hand-some boy seemed to smile and Bob smiled too and it was all smiles. Neither Simon nor his father mentioned it again.

It was a week before Simon was alone again with his brother. That week the word had become a mantra: secret and silent. Finally alone together he seethed the word through clenched jaw and teeth, up close, right in his handsome face, right in his well-turned ear. Called him spastic until the word was just sound, was as violent as a blow.

2

He has a single bag, all other belongings back in the cold of his Lambeth flat, unwatched, perhaps already robbed. He can hardly remember now whether he even Chubb-locked the door. Sure he did. A home invader's welcome to it all. Squatters will have to clean it up first. Take bleach to the toilet. Remove all his boxes and papers. Fumigate the sofa and bed. Weeks now. Should have given someone a key. Rented it out. Some time he will have to go back. Yes. Yolanda next door will keep a look out. He will go back some time and open the door and all will be the same. No power. No heat or light. But the same.

He sits on the edge of the bed. His is the cheapest room he could find. The junkies live here. The local junkies, not even the tourists. Thai rent boys. Thai hookers. Off shift, somewhere to crash. It is a place without conversation: just corridor nods, the meeting of tired eyes. There is a kind of cafeteria next door and his room backs onto its kitchen. He hears voices and the clank of pans all day and all night. He likes the percussion. He likes the simple, plain room. A mattress. His bag. Putty-coloured walls. A dim swinging bulb that jumps when people walk above. He preps the works, ties off, shoots and lies down on the slender bed.

His days have been the same since arriving. A routine. Picks up cash, walks the streets to the bar, has a beer, scores and heads back to the small plain room. An hour maximum. Perhaps not even forty minutes some days. How long, he forgets. It is not important.

Until the Christmas term he had been teaching at a primary school. Kids without English. Unable to read. Kids who looked blankly when you asked them a simple question. He liked to work with them. Their eventual comprehension. The slow, slow grasp of what was required. He tries now to stay away from those speaking English. Tries to be without understanding. Pointing, miming, shaking his head. He wants words to become useless, like his dead brother's limbs. Pointing, miming, shaking his head. Even the dealer says nothing now. Just palms the cash and passes the baggie. Simon orders his beer from the owner who doesn't speak a word of English. A routine.

At the primary school he'd met Anya. Underarm hair, dark crew-cut. Younger, somehow drawn to him. She invited him to her bare-boarded apartment, rag rugs, books and candles, and they talked all night. The next night they were naked together. He smoked some of her draw, did not tell her why he shouldn't. Smoked her draw and listened as she explained the way the world really worked. They did this many times, many nights. They lay in her narrow bed and he put his hand on her flat stomach as she raged.

'All the establishment needs is someone who doesn't realize the incredible hatred he inspires when on television. All the establishment needs is a stooge like that on the television and there's no unrest or upheaval. It's why game-show hosts move channels so often. They're making sure the hate never goes cold! They're making sure that just when you think you've got rid of one fucking prick, another one crops up in his place. One even more vacuous, even more slick, even more talentless than the one before.'

Simon had laughed then, and again now, remembering. *How I love you for this, how I love your overthinking mind. And how I love how you hate. You are talking about my father. You probably have him in your mind now.* He wanted to say this. He wanted her to know. But he just laughed.

'You might find it funny,' Anya said and turned from him, picked up the joint. 'But give it a decade, give it two, and the only assassinations will be of television stars. The so-called personalities will be terrified. Politicians will be safe. They will be able to do as they wish.'

Two decades and just the one assassination. A female presenter shot on her doorstep, a loner, stalker, caught: not what Anya had in mind. It changed the shape of his fantasies. He no longer imagined punching his father, shooting him, but dreamt instead of elaborate assassination. A snowplough accident. A dog attack in the middle of Hyde Park. A bomb placed in the annexe, timed to go off at the end of a playback of one of his game shows. Simon's preferred method was a piano pushed off the top of a tall building, crushing Bob below. Bob loves those old slapstick routines: let him die the way he has lived.

Anya has been on his mind since arriving in Thailand. Ghosts of her carrying a backpack, ghosts of her drinking beer in bars, ghosts of her rolling joints, scribbling in notebooks. She'd stayed at this same guest house. Cheap but fine. Cheap and close to everything. A higgle-piggle – when he thinks of her, he thinks of her saying those words – place with dank rooms and additions, enlargements and extensions leading into a garden courtyard where the chalets are. The chalets he'd looked at. They were not what he wanted. He liked the clatter of the next-door cafeteria, the low honk of voices, the pouring of liquid; the flames and fire.

'We'll go,' she'd said once, after a long description of Bangkok. 'You and I, we'll go together. Take the whole summer. Thailand, Vietnam, Cambodia. The grand tour. Temples. Meditation. Fresh seafood. The best hash in the world. A cabin by the beach.'

Anya, long limbed, naked, kissed him and he saw this would not happen. It did not. Years later, now perhaps, she would mention him in passing, at a dinner table, at work. With a father like that, she'd say – because now she knew, now she knew who he was – you can almost excuse it.

*

There is a photograph taken of the family. Not quite of the family. A photocall for the press. Father playing a miniature trumpet, mother with an admonishing, amused look that says *stop larking about*. Simon looking off with distracted eyes. His hair will not be tamed flat and his solemn look is directed at his off-camera brother. The handsome spastic is behind the photographer, no make-up applied, perhaps asleep, perhaps not.

'But why can't Gary be in the photo?' Simon asked. His father shot him a look and Simon said nothing more. He imagined killing Gary. Stabbing him with a kitchen knife, slitting his throat. Their father coming into the dining room to find Simon over the corpse of his brother, blood-drenched and smiling. Nine years old and thinking such thoughts. No wonder, when you think about it. No wonder.

He was a slight boy, but he managed to tip the chair just enough. Enough for Gary to fall, to dump the body onto the parquet floor. The noise was loud, like glass-shatter, and he paused over his brother waiting for footsteps on the stairs. There were none. He prodded his brother with the miniature trumpet. He pulled down his brother's trousers. He kicked his brother in the arse. He called his brother a spastic, a stupid bloody spastic. And his father and mother arrived then.

He wore his best clothes, the very best ones, the bow tie and shirt, the same he wore when important people came to the house. The nanny took him. A car drove them to a row of Georgian townhouses, brass plaques outside, steps up to shellac-dark doors, silver knockers and mother-of-pearl doorbells. He remembers the streets and the cars, the nanny waiting with him to be admitted.

But his memory of the sessions, even of the psychiatrist, is hazy: a book-lined room, a woolly headed man in tweed, horn-rimmed spectacles and a couch he assumed he was not allowed to sit on. Did he even ask to sit on it? This was a punishment, was it not? A punishment would not allow such comfort as sitting on its brown leather; he would not have asked, no.

And the questions. Have you ever wished to harm your brother? Have you ever harmed your brother? Have you ever wished to harm yourself? Have you ever tried to harm yourself? Give me three words to describe your father? What do you see in this picture? Can you tell me the first thing that comes into your head when I say these words: spastic, home, kiss, fear, anger . . .

They have the quality of a televised memory, shaped by dramas, documentaries he's seen. Did the doctor really ask whether he had hurt himself? Would a real doctor really ask about his father in such a way? Simon no longer knows. He cannot be certain. There were sessions; he's sure of that; and he remembers coming home to the quiet house, slipping in through the kitchen, hoping no one had noticed his absence.

For two months he didn't hear from or see his father. Not uncommon. But. Bob was touring, or writing for someone, or filming. Simon went to his psychiatrist appointments; did not call his brother a spastic. He did not kick his brother in the arse. He did his schoolwork and kept quiet, concentrated on his breathing as his counsellor had taught him. He ate his dinner, every last mouthful, and said please and thank you. He played well with others and he talked to Gary. He did not cry when the lights went out.

He was washing his hands, soap and water, water, soap and water, water. Washing his hands and his father was at the door. His father's face in the mirror, tired and lined. Simon dried his hands and his father stood with his arms outstretched.

'Come give me a hug, Simon,' he said. 'I've missed you my boy. Missed you so much.'

His father smelled of whisky and hair oil, his arms strong around him.

'You've been such a good boy,' Bob said. 'You've been such a good boy, Simon. That's what I've been told. I've been told you've been a good boy and every good boy deserves a treat. Come, come, Simon, I've a surprise for you.'

His father carried him to the study. In his arms and in the fervour of imagination, Simon seeing the surprises unfold, the sheer size of them, their frantic colours, their unknown, untold excitements. His father put him in the wing-backed chair. His father was smiling the way he did on the television when someone wins the big prize. His father handed him the brochure. A castle, something like a castle, green grass and turrets, but no moat or flags. In that moment, he is caught. This he thinks now amid the next-door voices and clanking. Caught in the moment of incomprehension. He is still there. Bob's face looking at him, the wrong face though; the eyebrows too arched, what looks like dried make-up on his chin and cheek. The smile dropped for an instant, then turned back on. The explanation. What he has won. A place at a boarding school. A permanent holiday from the family. Bob mentioned the sporting facilities many times, the cinema club every third Friday of the month. Your new school: didn't you do well?

The clank and voices. *Tak tak tak.* He picks up a bottle of lukewarm water. He is hotcold and sweating. The sheets are damp in places, wet elsewhere. He pissed the bed the first night of the boarding school. Pissed it so much the dormitory staff had to flip the mattress in full view of the others. Nine others laughing and calling him pisspants. Calling him pisspants though six of them had themselves been called pisspants before. He pissed the bed the second night too. The same routine.

'You need to sort yourself out, laddie,' the old woman said. 'Or else you'll be sleeping in your wet all term.'

The boys called him pisspants all through the third day. He did not piss the bed the third night. He broke one of the boys' noses. His blows were incredible. He heard one of the boys say, 'He's going to kill him! He's actually going to kill him!'

The dormitory staff wrested Simon from the boy, Simon still trying to land blows, blood on his knuckles, blood all over the boy's face. They locked Simon in a store cupboard for that. The teachers, not the boys. He was dry as a bone the next morning.

This room is bigger than the store cupboard, are there rats here too? The rats in the store cupboard. Yellow fangs, clutching cheese, their tails making Fu Manchu moustaches over his lip. What he told the boys. He preferred the store cupboard. To be told something is a punishment does not make it so.

Anya is next to him in the bed. Slender Anya, the coal of her joint burning red.

'We'll go,' she says, 'you and I, we'll go together. The grand tour. Temples. Meditation. Fresh seafood. The best hash in the world. A cabin by the beach.'

She smiles sadly and she has her hand out. Keys he puts there. Keys so briefly his, for the mortise and the latch. A key ring she bought for him that he had not thought to remove before giving them up. Cross my palm with silver. A door slams and the night is cold and he gets a bus home. He cries on the bus and no one offers him a handkerchief.

His father. His father Bob. Bob now in the corner of the room, standing in evening wear, dabbing a pocket square at the top of his brow.

'It's hot in here, isn't it?' Bob says. 'Good God it's hot. My wife'd hate it here. My wife can't stand the heat, you see. Can't stand the heat. I have to say though, it's a blessing: it keeps her out of the kitchen.'

Simon watches Bob wait for the laughter. Simon watches Bob wait for the applause. Simon turns over in the bed and closes his eyes.

3

Bob puts *The Flip Side* back unwatched and drags his fingers across the spines of the other tapes. Archivists' handwriting, not his own; the kind you see in libraries, in lawyers' offices. Were he to start now, Bob would not live long enough to watch them all. Tapes are stacked alongside the desk, last week's new recordings.

Behind an oil portrait of Jaq, the safe. He opens its combination lock. The numbers are not significant; there is no need for significance when you recall so much. Only important things. Only recall the significant things. A combination lock presents no challenge. But those things he considers not important slip through his fingers. Memory as value judgement. Memory as protectorate. He remembers as a child being fat. He remembers the Coronation Day parade, a Romany family passing, their caravan loudly painted, loudly hanging with Union Jack bunting, shouting something as he waved his flag, shouting Fatty Arbuckle at him, laughing and pointing. But he does not remember his mother pushing her fingers into his stomach. He does not recall her saying, 'You're a disgrace, Robert. Like a pig, always with your snout in the trough.' He does not recall his father laughing at him running in the park. He does not recall their comments to friends when all the kids were together. Mother and Father. Both dead now. No one now to say it ever happened.

The notebooks are the same shape and size: maroon boards, stitched. They have a fair weight, a solid heft. He takes them from the safe and arranges them side by side on the desktop. He sits on the leather-covered chair. He touches their covers, opens one and flicks through the pages, the cartoons and the jokes, the sketches and gags. At random: *People think I'm from Kent, I hear them say it as I walk past.* He looks at the line. Prestatyn, 1971, a motorway service station. Clumsy. He has used it many times, but it isn't quite there. Gets a laugh, yes, but clumsy. The forty-seventh page has five jokes about funerals. They are wretched. Written at this desk. Written after Gary's death and still in his black suit and tie, a bottle of Scotch and Jaq asleep.

*

He had not considered it an estrangement. Estrangement is for the upper classes, something they have been perfecting for centuries. The middle classes are made for reconciliation: even he and his mother made their peace in the end. At Jaq's prompting, a letter sent, a letter of admonishment and explanation, a list of questions he wanted answering. A letter came back, laced with cautious conciliation and ignoring the charges levelled at her. The summer of 1967. The summer of love. Three visits to her in Goring-by-Sea. Her in the rocking chair, the large gins and the cigarettes at her well-painted lip. Three visits and any mention of his wife, his marriage, its breakdown, waved away like trails of smoke. They talked a long time, but not of the cancer in her colon. They talked a long time, and he left for the last time. A coma. Reconciled and so now ready to die. Inevitable, the reconciliation. There could never be absolute defiance.

Absolute defiance. Yes. That was the look on his face, on Simon's face, walking up the driveway in his uniform, back from his first term. Bob had thought the boarding school would be the making of Simon. Something that would loosen his anger, strafe his resentment. A period of time away from Gary, some time for the boy to find his own voice, his own character. At the door, Bob welcomed him as the prodigal. Simon looked at him with the same look Bob had once tried to master towards his mother: hardened and uncaring, nonchalant about her disregard.

*

The intercom runs between kitchen and annexe, a speaker grille and push button screwed into the walls. Jaq calls him in for supper; she calls him in for sleep. She would rather not make the walk between the two buildings, rather not poke her head around the door. Though he does not say it, she understands she is intruding, even after twenty years. Having the space changed him. Jaq saw it straight away. Noticed it in his performances. Less polish, a slight easing of the worked-at patter. It looked like he cared less, like there was something perhaps more important than making those people laugh.

'You're more yourself now,' she said after a show in Bournemouth. 'You are more believable. More real.'

'Was I not before?' Bob said.

He looks up at her portrait, a good job. Captures her warmth and care, her smile. Lines had been smoothed, ridges of chin subtly excised. The woman the girl had promised. The girl in the office, one of the secretarial pool, typing and filing, making tea, booking tours. The office catered for well-to-do ex-servicemen, now turned comedy writers for hire. Young men, men in suits with cigarettes and constant back-and-forth, prising lines from one another, riffing, writing scraps down on fag-packets and bus tickets, the backs of menus, beer-mats. Their scrawl passed to Jaq and the girls for typing, the typed lines worked at with a pencil, then passed back to Jaq and the girls for retyping. A radio always on, the blast of the road beneath. The boys heading for the pubs, the boys heading for the restaurants, the girls never joining them, the girls preferring the singers and musicians from the offices downstairs. The songwriters and drummers, the singers and the promoters. Those men were distinct, aloof; hailing taxis, heading for cocktails, for all-night coffee bars. There were Negroes and Hispanics, Frenchmen and Americans. Next to them, the office boys were like the boys from school: sniggering, ill-informed, interchangeable. Jaq and the girls found their humour wearying; their bravado boring.

Jaq and the girls were young and slim; they breezed through rooms unaware these were the moments that would haunt them long into their lives: taking a glass of champagne from a silver salver, allowing their cigarettes to be kissed by offered lighters, spending their own hard-earned, heading home to their house-share in the Angel.

Unmarried and with lovers, unmarried yet not untouched. Later, looking back at photographs, their ghost selves alongside famous men who no one today would recognize, alongside nobodies who later were somebodies. Those dresses and hairstyles now back in fashion. Wondering what happened to the others, wondering what became of them all. All save Jaq.

Bob's memory elides the romantic and the documentary. He can recall the name and face of every woman he has ever slept with – Diane, Elizabeth, Suzanne, Angela, Kathryn, Emily, Susan, Mary, Liz, Linda, Pat, Deborah, Barbara, Karen, Suzy, Nancy, Anita, Donna, Cynthia, Sandra, Pamela, Sharon, Kathleen, Carol, Jenny, Cheryl, Janet, Kathy, Anna, Janice, Louisa, Yvonne, Victoria, Carolyn, Kathy, Jackie, Molly, Denise, Gill, Judy, Helen, Jean, Brenda, Linda, Tina, Margaret, Lorraine, Ann, Patsy, Tina, Rebecca, Bethany, Joyce, Helen, Tracy, Teresa, Wendy, Lizzie, Debra, Christine, Catherine, Amy, Sue, Linda, Leann, Shirley, Judith, Louise, Trudy, Holly, Mary, Lisa, Jeanne, Laura, Dawn, Gillian, Dorothy, Michelle, Sally, Victoria, Anne, Jayne, Phyllis, Elaine, Lois, Connie, Vicky, Sheila, Beth, Ann, Pat, Julie, Amelia, Gloria, Gail, Joan, Paula, Beth, Angie, Peggy, Cindy, Jennifer, Becky, Hope, Mary, Tina, Lisa, Pru, Kimberly, Martha, Jane, Cathy, Jo, Joanne, Debbie, Diana, Frances, Alice, Valerie, Marilyn, Ellen, Kim, Lori, Jean, Vicki,

Rhonda, Rita, Virginia, Katherine, Rose, Mary, Lynn, Jo, Ruth, Maria, Jacqueline – yet they are static memories. He can recall the couplings but not the feelings, not the reasons why some became affairs and others remained casual flings. An interviewer – no, more than one interviewer – observed that Bob wanted to please everyone. From street-sweeper to crown prince. He does not know what to make of that. A psychologist said it was all about his mother. There's a line in the sixth notebook, not his own: *That's the problem with shrinks, if it's not one thing, it's your mother.*

For years, Jaq worked beside him, day by day, night by night, until Bob was thunderstruck by her. Until his eyes were suddenly opened to her. He could not, could never, have thought this was possible, but yes, under his nose, all this time, all the time he had been embarking on futile affairs and diversions, been a bad boy, his angel was there all along. When he tells the story of their courtship, Jaq is struck by the grandness of his imagination. She does not recall it in any other way than his marriage ending and him casting around for a new wife. He bought her dinner. She was not the only one so treated. He does not recall this.

He remembers the cat-and-mouse game of her refusing to marry him. He does not remember her reticence at taking on the children, at becoming the new wife. It is a gloriously male, gloriously self-important narrative: the winning of her love, the finding of true happiness. Even between the two of them, when there is no one else to hear the story, he tells it the same way. Jaq does not correct him. There can be no correcting Bob's recall.

In the annexe, in the lamplight, Bob shuffles to the bathroom. He kneels beside the toilet bowl, its chemical stink, and tastes the whisky in his mouth. He is not going to vomit. He does not vomit. But he remains on the bathroom floor, his thin trouser seat on the carpet, his back against the wall. Simon is standing in the annexe. Simon, tumbler in hand, those stupid Lennon-glasses on, Bob sitting at the desk, listening. Simon has just come from the bathroom, a sherbet dab of powder on his unshaven top lip. Simon in the leather jacket and black denims, running a finger along the tapes on the wall unit.

This should have been a bust-up over money. This should have been a long rally of anger and resentment, the two men right up against each other, shouting. This should have been the words just under the surface, close up like veins, until a final, shuddering slam of the door. But instead it was a short, stilted conversation, barely remarkable. Barely something to recall.

'So how are you?' Bob watches himself ask his son the question.

'Fine. You?'

'Never better.' Bob watches himself shift. Weight from one leg to another.

'Anya?' he hears himself say. 'Is that her name?—'

Simon scratches his chin, wide smile that starts clenched in his jaw.

'Long story. For the best.'

'For the best, of course, yes. But, a shame, though. I know you were—'

'How's Gary?'

'He's wonderfully well. Doing better than ever.'

Bob remembers wanting Simon gone. The slight spin of the chair, the carelessness of his talk. Simon holding the tumbler of whisky and Bob having already finished his. A quick glance at the clock. Simon smiling, asking another question and Bob not hearing.

Bob watches the two of them talk. He sees himself looking at his watch and saying something about it being late, or last trains or something, Bob can't quite make out what is said. Simon is smiling, clenched again, and Simon is draining the glass. Simon is walking to the annexe door, where he pauses.

'Goodnight, God bless,' Bob says. It is a formal, stagey goodbye. Simon shakes his head and disappears.

A couple of days later the letter arrived. Long, tiny handwriting. The furies were in every line and every grievance.

. . . You sent me to the shrinks . . . boarding school, like Colditz it was . . . You called it a surprise . . . Way you treated Mum . . . months you were away and not even a phone call . . . a film more important . . . knew more about your contestants than me . . . can remember a script from a hundred years ago, but not my graduation . . . the only time your eyes widened was when I said I was going to go into entertainment . . . one word to the papers . . . the way you treat Gary . . . the way you use him . . . you are not there, are you? . . . The man who wasn't there, that's you . . . you hoard everything, but no one can hoard love . . . I AM NOT LIKE YOU.

Bob did not tell Jaq about the letter. He burned it a few months later. In the hearth, a murderer destroying evidence.

*

Gary died four years later, handsome, even more so laid out straight in the casket, peaceful and no strain in his face. Bob and his ex-wife had planned the funeral long in advance. Simon was to sit between Bob and his mother. There was hope there, the handsome son's death bringing the errant son back into the fold. In the church, father and son grieving together, arm in each other's arm, strength for the other's strength. A father and son, silently making peace.

At church, Bob greeted everyone graciously, but there was a space between him and his ex-wife. Bob refused to accept this as punishment. Bob cried for his dead, handsome son: gave thanks for a life almost lived. He did not look in the church for his youngest, though he saw him in every pew.

He and Jaq wintered in Barbados as usual. They ate lunch at their favourite restaurant. The two of them sitting at their table on the terrace; its rake and elevation perfect for looking out over the water's blue. Bob dressed like the off-duty captain of an ocean-liner: boat shoes and white trousers; something strangely commanding about his gait and bonhomie. A blue blazer, an Englishman abroad. Bob seeing Gary everywhere. Still missing Gary. Not a day. No. Not a day.

In the pall of Gary's death and in the hum of Simon's silence, there was a shift. A readjustment of culture: a searching back for something less complicated. Jokes that were just jokes. Gags that were just gags: no politics, no seriousness, no harangues. The national mood had turned nostalgic. Bob's act had not changed, nor his face, nor the oily, car-salesman smoothness his critics despised. None of it had changed, but the audiences swelled, and the plaudits and re-evaluations meant he was back on television, back telling jokes rather than filling time between rounds in a game show. He went on tour. Same gags. Exactly the same. About his wife. About airline food. About his sex life. One liners and stories. Songs even. Now a treasure. A young woman, dolled up like Dusty Springfield, a dress like those Jaq had worn when they'd first met, even made a pass at him. He'd laughed at the very idea.

'Now aren't you taking this retro thing a little too far, my dear?' he said as he saw Jaq walk into the bar.

*

With help from the toilet bowl Bob picks himself up from the floor. He finishes his Scotch and pours some more, settles himself again at the desk. The notebooks. The fucking notebooks. Everything from first to last. His true legacy. A shadow history of the world. What people laugh at, what they find funny. Is this not something to preserve, to cast in amber? The jokes working men tell each other, the jokes made at weddings, the jokes told to break the ice. How our bodies cause the most amusement, our shit and piss and cum. In these jokes, a whole history of how we live. Puns on advertising jingles, allusions to obsolete catchphrases, references to people no longer recognized. A history of everything. His life, yes, but everyone else's too, yes? A history not just of him, but of everyone else, of how we stay alive.

He puts both hands down on the notebooks. Cool and smooth. He opens them both. One page is almost unreadable, so small is the writing. He puts on his spectacles. There are lines spanning four decades. Lines written in three different continents. Lines written vertically and horizontally. Hands on the pages, where his hands had been before, different hands belonging to him.

He was putting the notebooks into his briefcase, late and waiting for the car. At their mews flat, cool and quiet, cooking smells from the oven. A bake of some kind. Later: good wine, music. Sinatra. Work now.

'I wish you hadn't gone,' Jaq said.

'I know,' he said. 'But what else could I do?'

She sipped her wine.

'I know you had to see him,' she said. 'I know that, I just wish you hadn't. All those years. All those years and then . . .'

'It was the filth,' he said. 'The filth of the place. It was disgusting. Dinner plates and papers everywhere. Bottles of milk. And he was just sitting there. Sitting there with those stupid bloody glasses on. Sitting there and smoking one after another. My son. Music so loud it was like it was playing in my chest.'

'You mustn't. You mustn't keep thinking the same things. Saying them over and over.'

'I know,' Bob said. 'I know, but you didn't see—'

'He wants to hurt you, love,' she said. 'You said it yourself.'

The car's lights caught in the panes of the kitchen window. Two quick blasts from the horn.

'I should go,' he said. 'We'll talk later.'

'Try not to think too much on it,' Jaq said.

A kiss and then the car through the streets, rain ditz on the windows, on the street. The buses, the cars, the orange-lamped cabs, all heading for Lambeth, for Simon. He took out the script, consulted the notebooks for comfort rather than inspiration. He knew the gags already; they were there. And then he was at the television studio, the lights full on and the cameras rolling and the first joke of the evening, polite laughter, a slight wave of the arm and on to the next. The stage doctor. The best palliative.

In the annexe, he turns the page of the notebook. Tight scrawl, a cartoon of a schoolboy. Hands that drew it, hands that wrote them. So many hands.

The floor manager and the producer, a few runners and a cameraman. The special guest and assorted uniformed people, looking at Bob. Everyone on the show looking. He remembers it well. A security guard in front of him.

'Overreacting? You fucking shit. I'll get you sacked for this. Overreacting? I never let them out of my fucking sight, you fucking little shit.'

And then in the greenroom, third Scotch and two

policemen, there on his insistence. Telling them all he knew: the last time he could be certain he had the note-books was in the taxi. Did they not see? A life had been taken from him, his life, a counter-life of the century. Did they not see what this was worth?

The next day, in all the papers, Bob. The next day, Bob offered a reward of £10,000 for the notebooks' safe and speedy return. The day after, a younger comedian offered a reward of £20,000 for them not to be returned. These, jokes.

4

He gets money, he goes to the bar, he has a beer and scores. This day, every day. Anya was in the bar. His mother. The parent who complained about him. The head teacher who fired him.

The school investigated, kept it quiet for all concerned. They found the kid was lying, but the reports on Simon were not good. The committee highlighted issues with his appearance and body odour, commented on his erratic moods. The way he worked with those who did not understand English and the way he worked with those who did.

'I am a good teacher,' he said at his hearing. 'Ask the kids. Ask them. Ask them whether I'm a good teacher or not.'

The three looked at him. The board of governors' committee. They talked amongst themselves. The decision was final. There was no pay-off. The following day they sent him his belongings, all of them in a red plastic crate. He was made to sign for them, a man with a chit shaking his head as he walked away. In the flat, Simon cooked up and took to his bed, the crate left beside the door.

There was money left. Money enough to get away. Not enough. When he was straight he checked the passbook. He went to the bank and they totalled up the interest. A few pounds, nothing more. An accumulation of pence on his £7,000 deposit. He went back to the flat, scoring on the way. He did the calculations. Enough for a year perhaps. Probably less.

In the small room, the clanking and the loud voices from the cafeteria next door, he thinks of shame. Those moments of shame.

His father's face on seeing the flat in Lambeth. This is where I live, this is who I am. Newspapers stacked. Paper plates. The living room overheated. Takeaway boxes, mouldy books.

'Jesus, Simon.'

'What do you want?' Simon said.

'What do I want? You called me.'

'I thought I was going to die,' Simon said. 'I wanted to see you before I died. But I didn't die. I didn't die, did I, Dad?'

And Simon rushed his father. Rushed him for an embrace. Bob faltered, stepped back.

'Are you on drugs,' Bob said. 'Tell me, are you on drugs?'

'I wanted to see you before you died. Or I died. Wanted to say see you in hell. Wanted to say fuck you, Bob. Wanted to tell you I hate you more than anyone else in this world.'

'I'm leaving,' Bob said. 'I thought—'

Bob left and slammed the door. Simon went to the window and opened it fully out wide. Three kids were by Bob's car.

Bob approached the car, the kids walked away. Something missed Bob's head by a matter of inches.

'You left your keys behind, Bob,' Simon shouted.

*

He bought kerosene and matches and a ticket to Egham. He sat on the train behind his Lennon-glasses. Kids on the train. Loud with patois, loud with their girls and their low-slung denims and fat-tongued trainers. Back-turned

193

baseballs caps and telling stories about fights and fucking up enemies. Talk of knives. Of spliff, the same kids he sees on the estate. The same kids he once taught, but unrecognizable. The kids who run errands for his dealer. The kids who would not recognize his father, just see another white man. Kids playing around, chin-ups on the handrails. One took an uneasy look at Simon. A quick glance. Whether it was worth fronting him. The kid went back to abusing his fat friend. Simon looked out of the window. Pimlico and the river.

In the shadows of summer, the long ones forming, the railway station. Did not hail a cab, walked to a pub and took a pint and sat in the garden. Smoked while people ate. Kerosene in his bag. He drank his pint and had a shot at the bar and another on the way out of the pub. The streets lined with trees, avenues you'd call them. He did not know this area well, just his father's house. He walked and could smell himself. The smell of his armpits. He smoked and walked. The kerosene. The matches: long matches, cooks' matches. Keys cut for the door, for the gates. Swiped from his father's coat and pressed into clay. Old Bryan, no questions, handed them over with a nod and a puff on his pipe.

Outside, the house was impressive: stuccoed walls, wrought-iron gates, a driveway crazy-paved. Daimler and Rolls-Royce in the garages. Personalized number plates;

as clichéd as you could hope. He let himself in through the back of the house, along the pathway. Were Bob and Jaq in they would be there to greet whoever he was; always a smile for a contractor, a workman, a caterer. Always a smile and a joke and kind word.

The first time he'd been to the new house – what he called new though they had lived there for over two decades – was for his father's birthday. He cannot recall which. The whole family, save for Simon's mum, Simon's mum now replaced by Jaq, sitting in the dining room. Simon sitting down, looking at his brother. In silence, always silence, chair-bound and still blessed. Simon beside him, left hand on the tyre of the wheelchair. The handsome fucking spastic. The whole family – spastic Gary, unwanted Simon, the stepmother – gathered in the large dining room, the father and husband opening a package. A present from Simon, bought by Jaq, wrapped by Jaq.

Bob took an age, saving the paper. A pair of socks, racing green, silk.

'Thank you, Simon,' Bob said and shook Simon by the hand. 'Is this your way of saying put a sock in it?'

Jaq laughed and Simon drank the last of the wine. The handsome spastic shifted in his chair.

'What's that, Gary?' Bob said.

'He says he wishes you'd put a sock in it,' Simon said. 'Even the deaf are sick of your voice.'

Bob laughed and picked up another present from the pile. It was a pair of leather gloves bought by Jaq, wrapped by Jaq, the tag saying with love from Gary.

'Oh now these are perfect, Gary,' Bob says. 'Just the ticket for when I strangle your brother.'

His father opened the last present, the one from Jaq. It was a long, thick tube wrapped in brown paper, tied off with ribbon. He put it to his lips. 'But, Jaq, I told you I was giving up.'

Bob struggled with the tape. Eventually the paper came away. An architect's tube, metal and plastic. Bob raised an eyebrow and cocked his head to one side.

Bob took the cap from the tube and shuffled out blueprints. They half unrolled and Jaq used ornaments as paperweights on the dining-room table. Simon joined them. He looked down as Bob hugged Jaq, hugged her tight and squeezed.

'What is it?' he asked Jaq.

'It's an annexe,' she said. 'Like an outhouse where he can watch all his films and things. A place where he can write. A place just for him.'

Simon looked down at the plans. Electricity and a flushing toilet. Shelves everywhere, an arched window looking out over the garden and pond.

'Like a sanctuary?' he said.

'Yes,' Jaq said, surprised. 'Yes, I suppose that's what it is.'

Looking at it then, low and squat, too white in the garden, too modern beside the mock-Tudor of the main house, Simon imagined what it would be like to have such a place at one's disposal. Such space, such quiet. A place only for you. His father took to calling it that, his sanctuary. Simon smoked a cigarette and watched the annexe. Strong door. Strong roof. The light was strong too, even at the last of the day, strong and almost purple.

He picked up the bag of kerosene and matches and walked the path. The key was snug in the lock and opened the door with a soft click, wood shushing over deep carpet as he pushed. Inside it was hushed, cool. A video recorder spooling. A television guide open on the sofa, programmes underlined, programmes ringed. The bathroom door ajar, the extractor silent, the stillness of it all. He sat at the desk. There were papers and correspondence. He would have read the letter here. It had got into his sanctuary.

Anya had ended it and his father had dismissed him. Sometime in 1988, the second summer of love. It was a litany, the letter. His failings as father and as man, all laid out, all the vitriol. *Anya said that you exist to be hated. You wish for love, but you do not deserve it, I am ashamed to be your son, ashamed to share your name. You only have one son, now, father. One son. And look at the state of him.*

Simon looked through the papers, wondering if the letter was there, still steaming in the stacks. There was no sign of it. Nothing. Simon stood and drank Bob's Scotch from the bottle. He cut out a line on the desk and then another. Above the desk was a dreadful portrait of his father's wife. Art as personalized number plate. All of this better-looking burned.

He walked along the stacks of tapes, the miles of cassettes, the neat handwriting, the chronological and thematic ordering. All this plastic to burn, tape bubbling, casing blistering, nothing left, nothing to salvage, atomizing into an acrid cloud billowing upwards. He took the kerosene and matches from his bag. He put them on the desk. He drank more Scotch and watched the light-sensitive lamps come on outside. The garden green and sculpted.

He ties off, shoots and lies down. The sounds from the cafeteria, the smells. He remembers the feeling. An ice line from neck to sternum, sitting in that annexe, a life surrounding him. He felt as executioner. He could take everything from his father. Every last thing. All that tilting at immortality, gone.

He remembers the moment of temptation. Imagining how it would actually feel to burn the place down. It had never been the plan. Just to seed the idea that he was capable of it. Just to leave the kerosene and the matches. To say: look at what I could do. But at that moment, in the annexe, the temptation. The devil on both shoulders. You will be caught, but do it anyway. You will be committing the ultimate betrayal, but do it anyway. You could run from the blaze laughing. Naked even. Yes. Naked and laughing, the annexe afire. You could run out naked and shouting, get yourself committed. You could drink more Scotch. All of his Scotch and fan the flames.

He looked at the clock. He checked his watch. He checked the clock again. He picked up the desk telephone and dialled his father's number.

'Dad,' he said. 'Dad, it's me.'

He could hear voices and shouting. The signal was poor and Bob sounded very far away, a small man at the bottom of a well.

'Simon?'

'Dad, I've done something, Dad.'

'What? What's that?'

'I couldn't do it, Dad.'

'What couldn't you do? Simon, what's going on?'

Simon started to cry. Good tears, well cried. Right on

cue. The runner closed in on Bob as he talked into the mobile telephone. Bob was pacing the corridor outside the dressing room. The runner took the notebooks from the open briefcase and walked away.

'I'm sitting here and I just couldn't, I didn't know what to do,' Simon said. He looked at his watch. Three minutes. He barely understood what he had been saying. He had been crying. He mentioned Anya. Yes. He mentioned Anya. He did not apologize. He's certain of that. He never apologized. Three minutes thirty and he hung up the phone. He drank the last of his Scotch and picked up the empty bag. He headed home with the annexe door wide, wide open.

A courier came the following day. Simon signed the chit and handed over the money in an envelope. Pick up and drop off. He took the notebooks and sat on the sofa. The untouchable books. Hidden on high shelves, dialled into wall safes, locked inside attaché cases. He liked the way they felt in his hand. The solidity of them. All the colours of ink, all the cartoons and doodles. He did not laugh. No laughter. Page after page, line after line, not one single laugh. It became a test of endurance. Two volumes to get through. He succeeded. A day or so and not a laugh.

His father's loss was on the television, in the newspapers. The heist of the century. The headline writers loved it. Bob was distraught, he made an appeal, as if a child was missing. It was the funniest thing Simon had ever seen him do. It still makes him laugh. Ten grand for the books. A reward! Ten grand for their safe return. Not for ten million. No. Not for a billion.

He sits up in bed and takes some water; his father is standing in the corner of the room.

'I have no regrets,' Simon says. 'Don't think I do.'

Bob pats his forehead with a pocket square.

'I'm not one for regrets, but I have one or two,' Bob said. 'I mean I bitterly regret that at seventy-four I can no longer have regular sex. These days I have to walk all the way to number eighty-nine.'

Simon lies on the slender bed, laughs silently.

5

The wine's pale burn in shimmer glass; the shatter glass of breaking waves. Bob and Jaq wintering in Barbados. Their favourite restaurant. He was standing by the large barbecue grill, the smoke beneath and the char on top of steaks and shrimp. Wine in hand, talking to the chef. The chef in the chef's hat, white teeth, dark skin – so long as they laugh, what do I care? – laughed and the boy waiters laughed with him, laughed at jokes old before their grandparents were born. The chef turned the meat and turned the shrimp and Bob was telling a joke about the Chinese. The maître d' waited for the punchline and, as the chef laughed, whispered in Bob's ear. Bob followed the maître d' to the telephone. His agent had the number, a few others. A boat horn blew, deep and baleful, a perfect summer's sound.

'Hi, Bob.'

'Pete?'

'I don't quite know how to tell you this.'

'Is everything okay?'

'The thing is, Bob. They found them. The notebooks. Someone's come forward. I'm at the police station now.'

'Have you seen them? Are they—?'

'They're yours, no question.'

'I don't believe it.'

'There's more to it than that though, Bob. Much more to it.'

Above him the clouds, sparse, and further out, the boat-horn sound of summer. What to say? Peter was speaking. He saw Jaq at the table, alone and looking out to sea. His chair pulled out, a waiter dancing past it. He listened to Peter and told him what to do. What he thought was best, what was best for Bob.

6

He gets money, he goes to the bar, he has a beer and he scores. This day, every day. This day he checks his balance. This day his balance is not as healthy as he had hoped. It puts the hex on him for the morning and he walks rather than goes back to the small plain room. He walks and there's too much spooling in his head. Too many things seen and unseen, faces poking out from behind bushes, legs and arms familiar but tanned. He walks until the bone itch is too much and then he is so far from home he feels he needs to shoot right there, but doesn't. Manages to keep the shakes and inner shits from taking over. Back to the room. *Tak tak tak* of voices, clanks of pans.

'Let's talk about shame,' Anya says in the bed. 'Is there any shame possible in this world? Any true shame? Does anything matter enough to feel shame about? You've read the Romantics. To feel shame, you need that surfeit of emotion. We feel guilty, we sense regret, but *shame*? Isn't this something we have lost?'

The needle is still in his arm, wagging. Shame, yes. Redemption, yes.

*

In a charity-shop suit, in the lobby of the police station, hair swept back into a lank ponytail. The specific smell of civic buildings: the same plants, same disinfectant, same chairs and tables. Simon sitting waiting for DC Watt. There are posters on a noticeboard. Message: you will be caught. Message: do report this. Message: we do believe you.

'Mr Connelly?' And so to.

He was taken into an interview room. Green walls, a blind, a tape recorder. The PC in uniform offered him coffee, which Simon declined. The suit smelled musty, but better than his own stink. He took the notebooks from the bag and put them on the table. The story. Run through.

Well, you see, I volunteer at a charity shop. You know, the Oxfam in Lambeth – true this – *and we have deliveries all the time. People come in, yeah. They come in and they leave the stuff by the door. So I was sorting the stuff out and I came across this box of books and other stuff and I saw these two notebooks. And I was going to throw them out, because who'd want some old notebooks, and then I looked inside and I saw. And I remembered. And I remembered the reward.*

The clock on the wall. White face, red sweeping second hand. Three grand by nine p.m. Eleven-thirty-six. In the a.m. This was shame. Ah yes, Anya, this was shame. His own fault. Brought on himself. A bad weekend. A bad couple of weeks. A bad month. On tick. Good for it. Always good for it. Not good for it. No more overdraft, no more credit. Bad debts to bad people. Not supposed to happen. Not to me. Others yes. Not to me. And the voice: there is always. No. Yes. The last thing. The only thing worth owning. The only things left not in hock. They were the very last things left. Not for £10 million, no. Not for a million, but for £10,000. For 10, of which he'd see only 7.

Two men entered the room. DC Watt and Sergeant Hoggart. They sat down. They pressed record on the tape recorder. They stated their names, job titles, and time. Eleven thirty-nine.

'Are these them?' Watt said. Simon nodded.

'I'm going to need to get these verified,' he said. 'Do you mind?'

'Not at all, I'm in no hurry,' he said.

They wrapped the books in evidence bags. Simon took cigarettes from his pocket.

'Do you mind?' he said.

'Not at all,' said DC Watt. 'Here.' He passed a small metal ashtray.

'So' – a look down to the notes in front of him, check

the name that does not need checking – 'Mr Connelly. Looks like you had quite a find yesterday.'

'It was something, yes,' Simon said. 'I still can't quite believe it.'

'Would you mind explaining to me,' Watt said. 'I know you've already given a statement, but I'd like to hear it from you. If you wouldn't mind.'

Eleven forty-six. Simon told the same story. Same words. Without inflection. Without impatience.

'Do you know?' Watt said to Sergeant Hoggart. 'You'll like this, you like a quiz, don't you, Frank? Do you know the one thing a newspaper isn't allowed to print in an advertisement for lost items?'

'I don't know, sir,' Frank said. 'But here's a guess: "no questions asked"?'

Watts thumbed at Frank.

'He's a clever bastard this one, clever as you like. He's right too. You can't just say no questions asked. Because it's like . . . I dunno, dealing with terrorists and hostage-takers: you're encouraging others to do the same. Commit the same crime. Theft for example.'

'I'm not sure I follow.'

'Questions need to be asked, that's all. Questions need to be answered.'

'I'm not sure how much more help I can be,' Simon said. 'I've told you all I know.'

There was a knock on the door. A lift of the blind. Eleven fifty-one. DC Watt stood. The uniform at the door whispered something to him. The blind rose again and fell.

'I'll be right back,' Watt said. Sergeant Hoggart paused the tape. Simon stubbed out his cigarette.

'Is this going to go on much longer?

'It'll take as long as it takes,' Hoggart said. Learned from a parent that voice, learned from a teacher. Simon looked at the clock. Shame. To lose this. To lose everything for so little.

'Would you like a coffee, sir?'

'No, I'd just like to know what is going on, please.'

'Won't be long now.'

The door opened. The blind opened and closed again. DC Watt came in holding a bag. Holdall, brown leather.

'Thank you for your patience, Mr Connelly,' Watt said. He slid the bag on the table. Tapped it with his right hand.

'All yours, Mr Connelly. Your reward.'

Simon stood and looked at the bag of money.

The needle is still in his arm, wagging. Shame, yes. Redemption, yes.

Watt looked at him, Simon looked at the bag. Three grand to pay off and then seven clear. Seven grand. Seven grand not to put up his nose. Seven grand to save. Seven grand to build up. Seven grand. A pitiful amount. Seven grand. If there were no threats. If it wasn't so far down the line. Seven grand. But something, yes. Something to begin with.

'Thank you,' he said. He walked to the door, the door held open by Watt. Watt smiling.

'Oh, by the way,' Watt said. 'Your father sends his love.'

Ah yes. Timing. A joke is all in the timing. Shame, yes. Redemption, yes. The inevitable reunion. Yes. His father in the corner. His father dabbing a pocket square to his forehead.

'It's hard to deal with death when it's someone close to you,' he says. 'You don't know whether to prop them up or let them fall.'

His father waits for the laughter. His father waits for his applause. Days later. Yes, days. Door kicked open. The needle still in his arm. Stiff. Let fall.

7

He can remember everything. A whole life, all of it. Every moment, every detail; every breath, every beat. Everything, all the way back to the moment of his birth. Sitting in the annexe, under lamplight, of this he is momentarily certain. The whole of his life. A whole life in a straight line from birth to death. How simple, how easy it seems, sitting in the annexe, under the lamplight. How simple and clear.

A video recorder begins to pull and wind; another stops spooling. He turns off the machines. All of them. He does not remember everything. He was not there. How could he remember? And now, he cannot even remember his son's face.

He turns seven pages and the third line is in blue ink, written while on a flight to Barbados. *I came home to find my son taking drugs – all my best ones, too.* He remembers the Lambeth flat. The photographs of the Thai hotel room. His letter. He remembers the absence. The phone call from Peter. What Peter said. He remembers Peter asking him what he wanted to do. Saying: are you sure? Peter saying: I can see him from here, from behind the blind. He remembers saying let him have it all, all £10,000. The bankbook, returned to Bob later. He remembers looking at it, up and down. He remembers the single deposit, cash £7,000, the day after the reward was paid. He remembers the way the money sat for years. The gradual accrual of interest, and then the first withdrawal.

He remembers a large withdrawal, the flight, and then the same amount withdrawn every subsequent day. He remembers what he instructed Peter to tell the police. He remembers clearly what he told Peter. Give him the money, Peter. Give him the money and tell him this. Tell him his father sends his love.

CHARTER YEAR, 1972

She had been told, tucked up, kissed goodbye: expected to rest. He had given her earplugs, placed them in the palm of her hand. Sleep, he'd said. You need it. Sleep. They were on the bedside table, sticky-ended with wax, slightly crushed. Her heart was audible when she wore them, an uncomfortable sound, so she'd taken them out just as soon as he'd inched the bedroom door shut.

Yvette's eyes were closed, better to concentrate on the pram-wheels scraping the hallway floor, his duffel coat being taken from the hat rack, the controlled rattle of the door chain, her child's choking sobs. She opened them as the front door quietly closed and, in her nightdress, hurried to the front-room window.

She leant against the sill and looked up the road, him and the pram under lamppost halos. The road was steep, winding; bungalows neatly spaced along it. She missed stairs. She missed height. And now she missed Owen, and their child.

While Owen tried to soothe Dylan, tried to stop his

constant screams with movement, she stayed by the window, waiting. She would not sleep. Could not: with the screams or without. It was more for him. For Owen. To make him feel he was doing something. On his return, she would pretend she'd slept. See him and the pram walking down the gradient, and then hurry to bed. He would come to the room and she would perform. It was an accomplished act: a stretching yawn, a quarter roll to the other side of the bed, an unnecessary 'What time is it?'

There were pills in the house. Bottles of them, brown like beer. The doctor urged her to take them. Sometimes she weighed them in her hand, but always put them back under their cotton wool. There were natural remedies too; herbal tonics and St John's wort. These she had taken in quantity, but their effectiveness was minimal. This wasn't something she liked to admit. She told Owen that she was fine. Just tired. Be better with rest.

He would come home from work in the car and busy himself with their son. He'd kiss her and ask her seriously about her day. She'd talk about Dylan: his bowel movements, his sleep patterns, his brief moments of quiet. And Owen would say, 'But what about you? How have you been?' At this she'd seethe, make claws of hands. His understanding, his kindness, his patience! And she would say, 'Fine. I'm fine, my love.'

His smile would be perfect. It told her flatly of her

own, singular failures. She watched the road for a long time, then saw Owen at the top of the hill. She took herself back to bed, quickly stepping through the house.

*

A car had pulled up outside their bungalow. Owen had seen it overtake them at the top of the hill and surprisingly stop. Its interior light was on, the engine idling. Dylan was finally asleep in the pram and Owen was careful to keep a steady speed on the way down, avoiding ruts in the pavement, the occasional patches of ice. When he reached the third lamppost, he recognized the car. It was a Jaguar, an older model: racing green, creamy leather seats. He quickly pushed the pram past the car, the door opening as he passed.

'Mr Coville?' The man smiled. 'I saw you on Moody Street. You passed my house. I would have called but I don't have your telephone number.'

'We don't have a phone, Mr Stevens,' Owen said.

'No. Of course not. How silly of me. May I come inside? I need to talk to you about a few things.'

'We were just going to get the little one off to bed, Mr Stevens.'

'It won't take a moment,' he said, getting out of the car and putting on a hat. 'Won't take any time at all.'

Stevens was tall, taller with the hat. He picked up an

briefcase from the passenger seat. Owen looked down at Dylan and waved Stevens towards the house.

'That's a beauty,' Stevens said pointing at the car on the driveway. 'French, is it?'

'Swedish,' Owen said. 'A Volvo.'

'I only buy British myself,' Stevens said. 'You always know where you are with a Jaguar.'

Owen nodded and opened the door. Yvette would pretend to be asleep. He wondered how long she would keep up the pretence. Long enough, he hoped, for Stevens to be long gone.

*

Dylan was born to the sound of fireworks and firecrackers, a few moments after the turn of 1972 – the seven-hundredth anniversary of the town's charter being granted. There had been complications. A caesarean section required. It would have been a natural birth, home conducted and drug-free. But instead, Owen had stood in a waiting room, drinking coffee, making small talk with a man from the town. It was the man's fourth and he had not been present at any of the births. He was red-faced and swaying drunk. Without Yvette's complications, Owen would have been there when Dylan was born, and this man's daughter would have been the baby on the front page of the local newspaper. The headline: 'Charter Baby Arrives Right on Time'.

*

'I've been to India,' Stevens said. 'During the war it was. Hot. Damned hot.'

He was standing next to the crammed bookshelves, holding one of the small Vishnus. Most of them had been bought at a head shop in Liverpool.

'Yvette and I went after university. We stayed on an ashram. It was quite something.'

'Is that right? There's an Indian family in town now, you know that? Moved here from Stockport. They're opening a restaurant, so I hear.'

His accent was neutral; unlike any Owen had heard in the town. He sat down. Stevens' briefcase was filled with paper, his handwriting all over them.

'Sorry, Mr Stevens—'

'Ron, please.'

'Sorry, Ron, but Yvette is sleeping and I have to get the dinner on . . .'

'I completely understand. New family, new pressures, what? I just want to run through some things with you.'

He passed over a carbon-copied sheet of paper. Names and dates. Times and schedules.

'This is of course only a provisional list of engagements, but I think all the major ones are covered. It's nothing too arduous. Just turn up, pose for a few photographs, then a meet and greet, as I like to call it. Shouldn't take more than an hour or so.'

Stevens smiled as Owen looked down the list, the ink smudgy and the paper thin. There was at least one event every month, with several clustered around July and August. Owen rolled a cigarette as he read down the list once, then twice. He lit the cigarette and shook his head.

'I'm sorry, Mr Stevens, this just won't be possible. We might be able to do some of these, but we have commitments and people to visit. And that's not even thinking about the strain on Yvette and Dylan.'

Stevens took the spectacles from his nose and wiped them on a spotted handkerchief.

'I do understand,' he said. 'But there isn't much I can do. I said at the time, believe me I said to the committee when they were programming this, that it was one heck of a schedule. But there wasn't anything we could do. It is what it is. And I did explain when we gave you your prizes that you'd be expected to join in the festivities.'

'You didn't say it would be a year-long commitment, though.'

Stevens hitched up his trousers. 'The town takes Charter Year very seriously. We've been planning this for five years, if you can believe that. It might be difficult to understand for those new to the area, but this is the most important year in the town's history. The Queen is coming to visit. *It's a Knockout* is being filmed here. It's a chance to really put us on the map.'

The smoke obscured the flash of Owen's smile. He had met Yvette on an anti-Vietnam rally. They had demonstrated on countless protests, joined underground political parties, smoked opium with poets. They were living in a bungalow, loaning out their baby for Tories to kiss and a monarch to hold.

'We can't do it,' Owen said. 'I'm sorry.'

Stevens stood and went to the window. He twitched the curtains.

'It is a nice motor, isn't it? Must be practical too, what with having a new child as well. I notice you drive it to work too. I see you as you pass of a morning on the way to Bateman's. Mr Bateman is a good boss, isn't he? He's a good friend of mine too, is Ken. A good friend of the town. His family's been here nine generations, I believe.'

Owen laughed. 'What are you trying to say, Stevens?'

'Simply that there are legal considerations – the car was a prize contingent on your being involved in Charter Year. And there are other things to take into account, too. Your standing in the town is very important. Not as important as your livelihood, but still . . .'

Stevens had left the curtains open. The Volvo had mud around the back tyres, but the rest of the bodywork was clean and polished.

'You can't take the car.' It came out so quickly, it surprised even Owen.

Stevens rubbed his hand over his chin.

'Farmer's were very kind to donate it as a prize. They want you turning up to all the functions in it. You must understand the predicament?'

Owen put out his cigarette and stood.

'This is ridiculous. We didn't even enter the prize! You just turned up with a photographer and that was that.'

'No one thought for a minute that you wouldn't be honoured, you see, Mr Coville. Nick Jervis was most disappointed to miss out. And to someone who's only been here five minutes too! In the circumstances, it really ought to be him to have the benefit of the car. Especially as there was some controversy—'

'What do you mean, "controversy"? Because Yvette had to have a caesarean? Are you serious?'

'All I'm saying, Mr Coville, is that there are options. Other people who would be more than willing to take your place. We don't want to do that, but it is an option. Just work with us, Mr Coville. Please.'

The door to the front room opened. Yvette was dressed in slacks and a blue blouse, her hair short and combed.

Mr Stevens half rose from the sofa. Yvette ignored him, bent down to kiss her baby, then kissed Owen. She offered her hand to Mr Stevens, then offered tea. Stevens declined.

'I couldn't help but overhear, Mr Stevens. Would you mind if I saw the schedule?' she said.

Stevens passed it to her. She held it in one hand, the other circled around Owen's waist.

'Owen is very protective of me,' she said. 'I've not been well since the birth. But I'm better now. And this all seems fine to me. I know we've not been in town for very long, but we love it here. The people are so friendly. And I promise we'll do everything we can in this very special year for the town.'

She squeezed Owen just below the ribs. Mr Stevens smiled, exposing his stained teeth and greying tongue.

'Are you sure, Mrs Coville? I don't wish to pressure you.'

'No pressure necessary. It would be an honour. But we do need to get on. I'm sure you understand.'

'But of course. I'll leave you to it.'

He stood and peered down into the pram.

'Beautiful little thing, isn't he?'

'We think so,' Yvette said. 'I'm sure the town will too.'

Stevens picked up his hat and retrieved his coat. From the car, he waved with gloved hands and sped away.

'Honey—'

'Shhh,' Yvette said. 'Don't worry, love. It's all okay.'

They embraced until Dylan woke. Dylan woke and began to scream. He screamed as Yvette picked him up, screamed as she kissed him, screamed as she tried to calm him down.

She took him into the bedroom, tried to get him to take a breast. He screamed and screamed, then suckled noisily.

'We're going to have some fun, you and me,' she whispered to him, stroking his downy head. 'It'll be a year no one forgets.'

Dylan screamed as she put him down. He screamed as she sang him a lullaby. He screamed for a long, long time.

SWARM

He was, without doubt, the most boring person she had ever linked. This she realized the moment she found him. An accident, that. She'd searched for *reading, physical* and his was the only link available. Usually he wasn't one for books, but at that moment, at that time – late on a Thursday night after she'd linked a woman who knitted a little too furiously – he was turning the pages of an operating manual. This is how she found him: reading an operating manual for an old coffee machine. *Please follow steps one thru five*, Deanna linked him read, *and prepare to enjoy coffee.*

The English was poorly translated, stiff and overly literal. It did not bother him. He was not amused by the manual's language; he simply read the words and turned the pages. He was standing in the small kitchenette. Orange cupboards, two-ring stove, fridge-freezer. The coffee machine was out of its box, its constituent parts laid out on the counter top. She linked him imagining the coffee machine in its finished state: interlocking pieces of chrome and glass and plastic. It gave him no satisfaction. The absence was seductive. She linked him build the machine, the following of steps one thru five. The pieces took some coaxing, but eventually he won out. It was finished, complete in the way he had imagined it. He did not smile. He did not even puff out his cheeks.

She linked him grinding coffee beans and filling the machine's reservoir. She anticipated a feeling of accomplishment, a small shiver of interest as the water began to bubble. But she was mistaken. She linked the smell of the coffee. It was heady, but his only reaction was to think of a cafe where he often ate lunch. She linked him watch the carafe fill and then linked him pour the coffee into a small mug. He took a sip. He took one more sip. It was fine. The machine worked. He poured the contents of the carafe and the mug down the sink. He removed the filter paper and emptied the grounds into the bin. He looked at his wristwatch and then at the machine, then again at his wristwatch. He washed out the carafe and set it down on the draining board. He dismantled the coffee machine and put the parts back in the box. He dried the carafe, put it in the box, and turned out the light.

He moved from the kitchen to the living area. The flooring was pale laminate, the walls whitewashed and unadorned. One screen. One window. One sofa. She linked the smell of a house cleaned once a week; once a week and thoroughly. She linked his every thought as he walked through to the small bathroom.

I have enough food for the next two days. I will order more on Saturday. The bins must be taken out tomorrow. My swimming shorts are dry.

He removed his clothes and brushed his teeth. She linked him urinate and wash his hands. He looked at himself in the mirror, but not for long enough to fully appreciate his appearance.

I will swim tomorrow and afterwards eat at the cafe. A man is coming tomorrow for the Dyson. Mr Martins. He will be interested in the Dust Buster too. I will settle for €2,000. No less. I should call Dad. I will call him tomorrow.

He thought the last of this as he got into bed. Cool sheets, clean pillow slips. There was a suggestion of prayer, just the movement of lips, but the words were so quickly skipped that Deanna couldn't be sure. He was asleep in a matter of minutes. There were no images before sleep; no dreams followed. After an hour of his sleeping, an hour of sullen, absolute still, the link went down.

The uLINK suggested adding credits to access David Collins' profile, his saved experiences, his recorded memories. Deanna was about to add the credits when she saw the stats. She had linked David Collins for seven hours straight. Even as a teen, she'd never made it past three. She understood what this meant. It could not mean anything else. It meant that she was in love with David Collins.

*

Deanna's first link was a girl called Shirelle. All the girls linked Shirelle; she was the hot link that summer. Twenty-two years old, a body lean and poised as a dancer's, dark hair piled into Mickey Mouse ears, a cigarette blazing. She was a runner in heels, a siren to write a song for. Joy, Rita and Ella had been linking her for months; Deanna a matter of weeks.

'We're lucky to have her,' Rita said. 'There's no one quite like Shirelle. There's never been anyone quite like Shirelle.'

'Expensive, though,' Ella said.

'She's worth the credit,' Joy said. 'So worth it.'

'There's no way she can survive, though, is there?' Deanna said. 'There's no way she's going to get out of this alive, is there?'

They were sitting in the communal gardens under the sun awning. Her three friends looked at Deanna.

'Of course not,' Rita said. 'And it'll be soon too. You've linked her. You know. We've just got to hope we're linked when it happens. It's like the ultimate trip, apparently. The dying.'

'Who says?' Deanna asked.

'Everyone says,' Rita said. 'Absolutely everyone.'

In class, on the way to class, on the shuttle bus from the estate to school and back, the only name she heard was Shirelle's. The students and teachers discussed her previous night's exploits – coke and weed, drink and sex, two men taking her at the same time – and whispered their predictions, how long she could hold out. The cost of the credits continued to escalate. Shirelle couldn't stop. Shirelle couldn't resist doing what they wanted.

Each time they linked her, they linked her tiredness. They linked her desperation. They linked her miscarrying. They linked her injecting opiates for the pain. They linked her abandoned and wandering the streets, bottle in hand, dressed always in her trademark fake-fur coat. They linked her shout at the moon – 'Please deliver me, please' – and then suck off a taxi driver because she'd lost her purse.

One night, unlinked and showering, Deanna was reminded of a parable, though she was unsure when she'd heard it. An avaricious man is granted three wishes and requests three sacks of gold. The sacks appear but the third sack is only half full. Confused, he sets about filling the sack with more gold, but the sack never seems closer to being full. The pursuit of filling the sack consumes the man, and he ends up a beggar, obsessed only with his half-full sack of gold. Deanna saw the man in rags, by the side of a dusty, biblical road, begging for gold. Behind him, Shirelle smoked a cigarette, drank from a bottle of vodka. Deanna wondered whether she'd misremembered the parable, or whether she had invented it.

Over five million linked Shirelle. The cost of credits jumped again. Jumped every day. They linked her, all of them, all five million, and they linked a birdlike heart, the acid reflux, the stumble out from darkness to light. They linked her from bar to pub to club, from scoring to sex, from passing out to dry-mouthed waking. The estates were alive with her. And when it became clear, when the depletion and tiredness was obvious even to Shirelle, people shut down their work for the day and hit the link.

Shirelle was already in the ambulance when Deanna linked her. Sirens and ticks and hums and beeps surrounding her. Declan, her friend with the calming hands and soft Belfast accent, sitting beside her. Deanna linked the first of the missed heartbeats. They all linked the missed heartbeats, they all linked the slow, slow realization of death. They revived her, they lost her, they revived her, they lost her. Then the link went down. The link went down and the music began to play. Something orchestral. Something specifically composed. Something written to amplify emotion. The credits rolled and Deanna dropped the link.

The messages from Joy and Rita and Ella began to flood her timelines.

*

Deanna woke early with thoughts only of David Collins. She messaged her boss to say she would be unable to work. She changed into her running shorts and T-shirt before realizing her usual routine would expose her. She linked an Ethiopian runner instead, a spindle of a man punishing a dewy track at dawn. She linked his slow-twitch muscles, his thin spikes entering the rubber, the steady heart rate and the rhythmic breath. She lasted twenty minutes. She had a message from her father, concerned for her well-being. He asked if she was all right, he'd heard she was ill. She told him not to worry, that she would be okay after some rest.

Deanna went back to the uLINK, added credits and accessed David Collins' profile. Usually, she didn't bother with profiles. There was too much posture in them, too much selling. David Collins had filled out the bare minimum of information. The accompanying video was the standard hour-long interview, but David Collins did not push himself in his answers. He looked disinterestedly into the camera and gave his brief, almost brusque replies.

He was twenty-nine. Unmarried. No lovers. Sex three times in his life, with three separate women. Not much of a drinker. Not a smoker. No drugs of any description. His mother and father were no longer together. David Collins answered the questions in much the same way he'd constructed the coffee maker: effectively and with the minimum energy expended. The interview was designed to provoke emotion and memory, to flesh out a character, to give them motivation, to give them a sense of narrative. But David Collins offered nothing.

'Why are you here?' the interviewer asked last of all. Collins paused. He tapped his fingers lightly on the kitchen table in front of him. He took a sip from his small beaker of water.

'To be certain that I am here,' David Collins said. He smiled without humour or sadness. 'Isn't that why everyone's here?'

Deanna added further credits and booted up his 'selected recorded experiences' – an edited highlights package of what to expect from David Collins. It was the standard three hours, put together from the previous month's feed. She hit the link and settled down. She linked him walk the same eight flyblown and dusty streets, his pace slow and steady; linked him eat at the same cafe day after day, his over-salted lunches and dinners taken without enjoyment; linked him swim in a municipal swimming pool, his stroke rhythmic and concise; linked him selling faded-plastic heirlooms, his posture poor on a wood and wire chair; linked him heading to his small apartment each evening, his nightly routine of teeth brushing, showering and bed at a sensible hour. She linked him and felt absolutely nothing, not a thing.

But then Sunday – there were people outside the small church, their clenched fists and clutched Bibles – she linked him walk to another small apartment, a man opening the door, Collins' father, clearly, and the man inviting him inside. At the moment of the father opening the door, Deanna felt something shimmer. Not the *basso crescendo* when someone's emotions are fully engaged; something more like a click. An errant pulse, perhaps. She linked David having a drink, eating at the table, then getting up to leave. The next week was exactly the same. The streets, the cafe, the office, the pool, the apartment, and then the Sunday visit; the same every week.

The father, Paul, opens the door. David experiences the shimmer and walks inside. They enter the kitchen and Paul pours a glass of beer for them both. A shepherd's pie browns under the grill.

'So, how are you, son?' Paul says. 'Winning?'

'Fine, Dad. You?'

'Fine.'

They say the same thing each week. The same three lines and then David drinks from his beer, as though grace has been said. Lunch is served. They talk. About their week, their work. David loads the dishwasher while Paul wipes down the surfaces and table. They shake hands at the door, a handshake that turns into an awkward embrace.

Deanna had promised herself she would only go through the profile and experiences. She had been clear with herself. She would not waste her day, a day to herself. She would not stay on the uLINK. She would do something else instead. Read a book. Take a long bath. Call her father. But she clicked the live link anyway. Without thought or self-justification.

David Collins was standing in the kitchenette. She linked him as he replaced the cracked screen and processor board of a mobile telephone. It was painstaking, delicate work. She linked him holding his breath and releasing it. The repair took almost two hours, his fingers thin and the screwdriver tiny, like a jeweller's. She linked him complete the job, put the telephone in a box and turn out the light. She linked his every thought as he walked through to the small bathroom.

I have enough food for the next five days. The recycling must go out tomorrow. My swimming shorts are drying in the bathroom.

Deanna linked him until the feed went down. She went to bed and slept as long and as dreamlessly as David Collins.

*

Her father was dressed as though their lunch was important: slacks and a pressed shirt, polished shoes. Deanna was there already, which surprised him, and she waved – she had practised this – across the restaurant. He waved back and weaved between the round tables. She'd chosen the place because they'd once eaten there, years before, and she remembered the food was good, or the atmosphere was good, or was it the chairs? Something about it, whatever it was, was good. And sitting there in the late afternoon sunshine, crunching ice from her iced water, a thick cloth napkin and two perfectly transparent wine glasses in front of her, something about it was good.

'Well hello,' her father said, leaning down to kiss her. 'You look wonderful.'

'Thanks,' she said. 'I was trying to remember, though. When was it we came here? The two of us?'

'You and me?' he said, sitting down and placing his hands flat on the table. 'Just the two of us?'

She nodded. He picked up the menu, the paper rolled into a horn.

'I don't remember. Years ago, must be.'

'I remember there was something good about it. Something was good.'

'The fish is good here,' he said. 'Maybe that's what it is?'

'Possibly,' she said, though it didn't seem likely. It occurred to her that her father had no recollection of eating in the restaurant with her. She wondered what it would be like to link her father. What memories he would have, and how many would cross-check with hers. Her father smiled and held his hand out across the cream tablecloth, past the floral centrepiece.

'I just wanted to say —'

'Don't, Dad,' she said. 'You don't have to. Let's just have lunch. Just the two of us, a nice lunch. I'm going to have wine. Treat myself.'

'In that case,' he said, 'so will I.'

He talked of his job – he worked for the land registry – of lunches he had eaten, of the people from her past he had seen. She was encouraging and kept the conversation going. They shared a starter.

'I've met someone,' she said, halfway through her main course salad, interrupting her father's recounting of an intra-office feud.

'You have?' he said. He put down his cutlery, took a small sip of wine.

'Yes,' she said.

'Well, that's great, love. Great. What's his name? How did you meet?'

'I don't want to talk about it,' she said. 'I just wanted you to know. I just wanted to tell you.'

'You look happy,' he said picking up his knife and fork, his face slightly pinked from the wine and excitement. 'I saw that as I came in through the door. You look . . . contented. I can't tell you how happy I am for you.'

Deanna swilled the wine in her glass and looked at her father. Steely hair brushed carefully to a parting, an open-neck shirt, a small shaving nick under his left earlobe. She had expected to feel something as she told him. Happiness at the joy she'd provoked. Excitement at the sharing of a confidence. A cruel sense of deception. But she hadn't. What she'd said had been a simple statement of the facts. Or at least an iteration of the facts. Her father's reaction was not important to her. She might as well have been David Collins telling his father there was a buyer for a Dyson vacuum cleaner. The delivery was the same. The same distinct ambivalence.

Her father ordered another glass of wine. She ordered one too but did not drink it. She let him talk. She let him describe meeting her mother, the old story coming out again. His long, sorry romantic tale. She let him talk. She let him get to the tears in his eyes, let him wipe them on the thick cloth napkin, let him excuse himself to the bathroom.

*

Deanna told everyone she was going to the south of France. They wished her a pleasant holiday. They said it was a good thing to get away. She nodded and locked the door to her apartment and spent the next fourteen days with David Collins. Going to work, swimming, reading manuals, eating at the cafe, taking out the rubbish. She woke with him and slept with him, their two bodies in constant contact. She noticed a scar on his inside leg for the first time. She linked him change his energy supplier and buy a new pair of work trousers. She linked him talk to his father on the telephone and go to his father's house for lunch on Sundays.

That last Sunday, a message popped up on the interface. *David Collins has moved from basic rate to premium level one. Please add credits to continue.* She added the credits and continued. She linked him in his apartment, showering, the same as every other day. Soon she was leaving his apartment and walking to his father's house. But Deanna was unsettled by the message. The uLINK people had clearly seen she was hooked. They were going to extort her. They were going to punish her for loving David Collins.

David's father opened the door. David experienced the shimmer and walked inside. They went into the kitchen and Paul poured a glass of beer for them both. A shepherd's pie browned under the grill.

'So, how are you, son?' Paul said. 'Winning?'

'Fine, Dad. You?'

'Fine.'

Deanna linked him watch his father wipe the surface and table with a dishcloth. Usually he did this after the two men had eaten. The counter tops always stayed dotted with potato and meat until after lunch. She linked David watch Paul drink half of his beer in one lunge. She noticed Paul had also forgotten to put the ketchup and brown sauce on the otherwise-laid table. David took a sip of beer.

'I've got a buyer for the Corby Trouser Press,' he said.

'What's that?' his father said. 'What?'

'The Corby Trouser Press. I've got a buyer for it. Three grand, I think. Maybe more, I don't know.'

'That's great, son,' he said. 'Great.'

David sat down at the table as usual. But Paul was fussing and knocked a tray to the floor. It made a loud clang as it hit the tiles.

'Is something burning?' David said and pointed at the oven.

'Oh shit,' Paul said and wrapped his hands in oven

gloves. He opened the oven door and smoke stole out. When it cleared, the top of the shepherd's pie was sooty black. The smoke alarm was triggered. The noise was hectic. Paul stood on a chair and disarmed it and stood looking down on David. Deanna noticed David's heart rate was marginally higher, felt it rise and fall back to normal.

'Sometimes, Dad,' David said, 'you really are a bloody idiot.'

Paul got down from the chair. He stood with his hands gripping the kitchen sink. He was breathing heavily.

'Don't talk to me like that,' Paul said. 'Don't you dare talk to me that way in my own house.'

'Don't act like a bloody idiot in your own house, then,' David said. He got up and put on his jacket.

'And where do you think you're going?' Paul said. 'We haven't had our lunch yet.'

'I'm not eating that shit,' David said. He picked up his coat and walked out the door.

Deanna dropped the link. David Collins had been calm throughout. Calm and detached and yet. She saw the anger in Paul. The rage as David left. She went to the bathroom and was sick. She ran water and washed her face. She went back to the uLINK and stared at the interface. She was frightened to link him again. Even if David now stayed calm, she was not sure she could take it. She sat at the uLINK all afternoon, but did not connect. She just sat there, looking at the interface. For a long time, she couldn't think of anything to do that didn't involve David Collins.

Eventually she went for a walk, out into the communal gardens. She had a flavoured water sitting out on a cafe's terrace, and watched lovers and friends walk dogs or stroll towards the river. Everyone was talking. At all the tables around her, people talking and laughing. She left her drink and headed home.

She had a long bath. She dried herself and without thinking went straight to the uLINK. She accessed the saved experiences and selected a series of Sundays. Iterations without a hint of drama or conflict. *David Collins has moved from premium level one to premium level two*, the interface said. *Please add credits to continue.*

*

During the week she was struck down by a migraine, a migraine that lasted six days. A week of her bed, a week of sweats and shivers, a week without him. She told herself it was her body's way of telling her to stop. A side-effect of the linking. She hated her body. She hated what her mind was telling her.

By Sunday she was better, the pain lifting like morning mist. She woke early, before sunrise, and showered and washed her hair, exfoliated, toned, moisturized. She made coffee and drank it watching the sunrise. Then she turned on the interface. *David Collins has moved from premium level two to premium level twelve,* the interface said. *Please add credits to continue.*

At the height of her fame, Shirelle had made it to premium level twenty. Deanna didn't know how many levels there were, but that was the highest she had ever seen. She looked at the interface again. Premium level twelve. She swore vengeance on the uLINK people. They were bleeding her dry. She'd heard about people running up debts they couldn't pay, but couldn't imagine how. The terms and conditions were clear.

3.17 – The cost of an individual link can increase due to demand, either by an individual's personal usage or by increased interest from the uLINK community. You will always be informed of any change in pricing for a link.

Even after a week without him, they knew she would pay. She added the credits and linked him as he woke, as he walked from bedroom to bathroom.

It was a typical Sunday. She linked him take a shower, read a manual, walk to his father's house. Paul greeted him as usual, but paused before closing the door.

'So, how are you, son?' Paul said. 'Winning?'

'Fine, Dad. You?'

'Fine.'

She linked David drink his beer. There was a long and static silence. Paul drank his beer. She linked David Collins sitting at the table.

'If it's money,' David said, 'you know the answer.'

'They fired me,' he said. 'Someone had it in for me. That bastard Murphy. He's had it in for me since I got there. They said I didn't follow procedure. They said that I was sloppy. Me! That the team wasn't performing as projected. He had it in for me from the start, from the beginning—'

'Someone's always got it in for you. Always. It's never you, is it?'

'You weren't there. You didn't see what he—'

'The answer is no. How many times no. How much do you owe me already? Tell me. How much?'

Paul turned to the stove. He took the pie from the oven and set it on a trivet to cool.

'And you call yourself a son?' he said.

'I don't call myself anything,' David said.

*

All week she linked David Collins and for the whole week his heartbeat barely rose from normal. He reconstructed several new machines, of which he sold two without pleasure. He ate his dinner at the cafe and swam in the municipal pool.

The following Sunday, Deanna agreed to meet her father at the same restaurant as before. They sat at the same table. Her father was late arriving. He was dressed with precision.

'Well hello,' her father said, leaning down to kiss her. 'How are you?'

She saw concern on his face.

'Is everything okay?' he said.

'Everything's fine,' she said. 'I was just trying to remember what I had the last time we were here.'

'The fish is good here,' he said. 'You probably had the fish.'

'Yes,' she said. 'Probably.'

They talked politely. Him most of all. He talked of his job, of lunches he had eaten, of the people from her past he had seen. She kept the conversation going. They shared a starter.

'We split up,' she said. 'That man and me.'

'Oh, I'm sorry to hear that,' he said. 'I could tell something was up. I could just tell. From across the room.'

'I'm fine. I don't want to talk about it. I just wanted you to know, that's all.'

She had not known it was over until that moment. She expected to feel something afterwards. Guilt, perhaps, remorse, a sense of mourning. But no. A statement of fact. No more.

Her father ordered another glass of wine and she put her hand over her glass. She let him talk. She let him describe losing her mother, the old story coming out again. His long, sorry, romantic tale.

There were tables north, south, east and west of her: north and south with four diners; east and west with two. Her father absent, she toyed with her napkin and heard someone say the word Collins. She heard it again from the west and then from the north, from the south and then the east.

. . . he can't survive . . .

. . . but surely someone would do something . . .

. . . police can't, not without proof . . .

. . . you sort of can't blame him . . .

. . . he's a monster, if I raised a child like that . . .

. . . but I hear the father's involved . . .

. . . he started the rumours . . .

. . . to get the cash, to get his hands on his cash . . .

. . . it's clever when you think, really, getting all those followers for something that might not happen . . .

. . . it will happen . . .

. . . I find it so sad . . .

. . . I'd ban it. I've said it before . . .

. . . we'll be home, don't worry . . .

. . . they say it's the ultimate trip . . .

. . . it's the hype I can't stand . . .

Deanna stood. She was still holding the napkin as she walked out of the restaurant.

*

Shirelle had once said to Declan that you feel the weight of the links. Feel them at the back of your neck, like bees: like a swarm of bees. She scratched the back of her neck as she told him this. Scratched and said: 'You can feel the pressure. Like they're pushing and pushing until your whole head's just filled with bees. Buzzing with them.' Deanna had thought it was just the drugs. But she could link it in David Collins too.

Deanna linked David Collins walk the streets to his father's house. She linked him scratch the back of his neck, linked the pressure where once there was none. His heart rate was up and she could feel the agitation, the agitation in his arms and legs. She linked his rangy, erratic steps and saw his father's face at the door. Hair greyer. Face more ashen. His arms open: come on in.

She linked the smell of the shepherd's pie. They all linked it. She linked him hear his father say, 'So, how are you, son? Winning?' and she linked David reply. They all linked it.

She linked him drink his beer. They all linked it. She linked him sit down at the table and eat his pie. She linked him loading the dishwasher. They all linked it.

She linked the kitchen knife entering his gut. The twist of it. The blade cold and the flesh burning. She linked him looking at his father's face, blood on it, blood everywhere. Arterial spray. She linked the blade being removed, and then entering the gut again. She linked David Collins bleeding, the blood pooling on the floor. They linked the pain, the astonishing pain. They all linked it.

She linked him watch his father standing, bloodied, a face gone from rage to terror. She linked David Collins smile. And then there was nothing.

Deanna's link went down then. Everybody's link went down. Deanna heard the music. Everybody heard the music. Deanna saw the credits roll. Everybody saw the credits roll. Deanna thought of David Collins and Deanna began to cry.

Deanna cried and it was glorious.

THIS IS NOT A TEST

Because he loved her still, in the end he let her win. It was not a battle of wits: she had just decided that it was time and once she'd decided, he had just the pretence to go through: the changing of the subject, the grudging acceptance, the putting off of the booking. He delayed and prevaricated, made his excuses, and then they were at the airport, and then on the plane, and then in the air.

Don never discussed home with Maggie, only with patrons and holidaymakers. They'd sit at his bar and tell him he had it right: away from the weather, the people, the traffic. They'd tell him they wanted to pack it in and sell up like him, to open a bar by the beach like him, drink free-poured vodka-tonics all day long like him. Holiday talk. Sun-drunk talk. Drunk-drunk talk. Sentiments as forgettable as a round of drinks. He'd smile. Pour them shots. Empty salty popcorn into plastic-wire bowls. Tell them they were lucky to be able to go home. To leave Cyprus. That he missed home so much. No, seriously.

I do, I miss the old place. Then laugh. Laugh and slap his hand on the bar.

The aeroplane banked, dropped and juddered. He had been flatulent on the flight and he felt an uncomfortable settling in his gut. Their big suitcase was old-fashioned and too large for the overhead lockers, but he had refused to buy a new one. They would be made now to wait at the baggage reclaim and his own stubbornness irritated him.

Before the seatbelt light was extinguished – against the instructions of the pilot and the steward – passengers were on their feet. In the gangways people dithered, blocked others in, held up the line. Contained rage is the overriding modern emotion. You feel it everywhere. Gibbs had said that. How many years ago now? Don had not agreed then, but waiting to disembark from the plane he understood what Gibbs had meant.

He and Gibbs had started work on the same day. In separate rooms, in different council buildings, they signed the Official Secrets Act and were taken to the Bunker. They met in the induction, in the briefing room beneath ground level. Five chairs in a low-ceilinged antechamber and an operational map behind a lectern. Some joke shared together, something that Gibbs said to make Don laugh. Then the speech from the captain. First line of defence. A Cold War we will not lose. Victory from the jaws of Armageddon.

The Bunker had been built at disproportionate expense, one of eleven secret facilities across the country, set deep and safe into the Cheshire plains. It was built for when the bombs would come: one hundred and thirty-five people – military, political – would shelter there; one hundred and thirty-five working towards keeping order, broadcasting essential information and encouragement to survivors. It was 1978 and he and Gibbs and two others were seconded from their posts. They would be setting up the communications systems. They would oversee the entire enterprise. They spent sixteen years there in the end. Testing equipment, running diagnostics, taking part in endless drills. They were young men but aged quickly. Neither had children. Neither wanted them. Don's wife said she understood; Gibbs' wife said she did not.

Don watched Maggie talk on her phone. She was standing by the baggage carousel while he waited, hands tightly gripped on the trolley. Slender still, her grey-honey hair in a band. White T-shirt, cardigan and culottes. Sensible shoes she'd replace with a showier pair before walking through customs. Over their years together she'd retained her accent and he had almost lost his. Scottish her; Midlands him. He was thankful it was that way around. Her voice aroused him. They were that kind of couple: middle-sixties and still with the shock of lust about them.

In the arrivals hall Maggie's son, James, his wife and their daughter were waiting for them. In Gracie's four-year-old hands was a felt-tipped sign: Nanny Mags + Poppa Don. There were loud greetings, awkward laughter. James shook Don's hand. James's wife, Andrea, kissed Don's cheek. But when Don bent down to hug Gracie the child turned quickly back into her mother's denimed leg. Don laughed. He told Gracie he'd get her later.

'Good to see you, James,' Don said.

'You too,' James said. 'Welcome home.'

Don had only ever seen James when he'd come to visit them in Cyprus. His stepson would always arrive with a sneer about him, a condescending sniff at the clientele in Don's bar; at the pub quizzes, at the bingo sessions. Had Don ever had children, had he responded to his then-wife's creeping silence, he knew he'd have ended up with a boy like James. Politely distant. A sharer of small talk. A man of average height and intelligence who, despite his own limitations, would manage to convey an air of modest amusement towards his father.

It was cramped in the car with the child-seat wedged between them. The windows fogged and Don wiped the glass to see the other cars and drivers, the new superstores and drive-thrus, the illuminated signs on elevated poles.

'How long's it been, Don?' James asked.

'Twelve, no, thirteen years,' he said.

'Far too long,' Maggie said and put her hand on Don's thigh.

Don looked out of the window. Maggie and he used to drive across the country in separate cars to a common destination. City breaks: Dundee, Hull, York, Bristol. Anywhere she could claim as a business trip. One night and then a day of walking, holding hands, kissing outside galleries and local places of interest, until the next day they ended up back at their adjacent cars, rain maybe falling by now and dampening their clothes, saying goodbye again.

For their more regular meetings they'd found a hotel twenty-five miles from her house and twenty-one from his. It was an ugly building even for the seventies, and it was there they'd called an end to the affair. That day should have looked more like the one he saw now, out the window of James's family car: sink-grey skies and belts of rain. Instead it had been pleasantly hot, and they'd agreed that it could not go on, knowing this was untrue and yet true. They said goodbye and drove away and he could not remember where he had driven to, how long it had taken to make it back to his wife.

That same hotel had almost caught them out. Don had been distracted after paying and had put the room receipt in the hip pocket of his jacket. Jayne was not a suspicious person – she had a faith in Don that he found defeating – but had come across the slip of waxy paper while hunting for a lighter. She looked it over and left it on the kitchen table for him to find. He spotted it as he was pouring himself a drink; he picked it up and it felt icy to the touch.

'Where did you find this?' he said. Jayne turned from the chopping board on which she was heading lettuce.

'In your grey jacket,' she said.

'Thank God!' he said. 'We've been looking for that all day. I must have picked it up by mistake.'

Jayne put down the knife. 'You were looking for a hotel bill?'

'Anderson had to stay there the other night. Just come down from Strathclyde. He's been in a terrible state about it. Without a receipt he can't claim it back on expenses.'

Jayne nodded.

'You'd have thought they'd put them up in a better hotel,' she said. 'That place is a monstrosity.'

They pulled off the motorway. James and his mother were chatting; Andrea was on her phone. Don tried talking to Gracie, but the child ignored him. He had an itch around his throat. He scratched it, the noise coarse. Gracie looked at him. Donald smiled and frowned and gurned and made some experimental noises. For a time, she was diverted; then she looked away and he was pulling faces for no one.

Years after the affair and his marriage were over, he discovered Cyprus. Barry – a co-worker from the Bunker – had moved there after his wife died. His bones had always felt the cold, he explained in a letter to Don, and the heat of Cyprus was something else. But he missed the old times, missed his war buddies, and so he'd invited him over to catch some sun.

Barry had picked him up from the airport and driven him to the resort. A little England. The cafes and bars. Small shops with racks of the *Daily Mail* and the *Sun*. Televisions showing football matches and the soaps at off-schedule times. Traditional home-cooked food alongside specialities of the region. HP sauce on the tables. Salad cream. PG tips. Barry thought it was perfect. Barry stood up for the national anthem. Barry liked talking to Americans because they understood about taking pride in your country. Donald resisted asking Barry why he'd moved away if he loved his country so much.

'This is new, isn't it?' Don said to James as they took a right turn. 'The bypass?'

Don couldn't recall what had been there before. Waste ground, houses, factories, something anyway. The edge of town, just off the motorway, a few miles to his and Jayne's old house and in the opposite direction, Maggie's.

He looked at Gracie and she looked back at him. Just for a moment. Then she looked out of the window.

They ate an Indian takeaway at James's dining table, Gracie already bathed and in bed. This was what Maggie always did when she came to see her son. The house was newly built and perfectly situated for a new family. The beer wasn't cold enough and Don had lost the taste for curry. He ate slowly. No one noticed his quiet, not even Maggie.

In the night Don woke, uncomfortably full, and sat for a long time in the bathroom. A thick book was set on top of the cistern, an encyclopaedia of trivia and facts. He held the best pub quiz in the resort, no question. Regulars knew the answer to the last question was always 'Sweet Caroline'. The bar would rise in song, Don leading them through the chorus.

He thought of Elvis reading *The Scientific Search for the Face of Jesus* as the King crapped out the last of his life. He put down the book. Pulled up his pyjama bottoms. Looked at his watch.

The Bunker had opened to the public the year before. There had been a gala reception and he'd been sent an invitation. Gibbs called to convince him to come; it had been too long, they hadn't seen each other in a decade. Maggie had tried her best to convince him too.

'When do we ever get invited to a gala anything?' she

asked him. 'Will we ever get invited to anything like this again?'

'I said no and I mean no,' he said. 'I don't care if the Queen and the Red Arrows are there. No.'

He started to dream of the Bunker after that. Months of dreams of its telephones and computers and static. Of coming home to Jayne as she peeled potatoes for dinner, the shower he took to wash off the smell of the Bunker, or of Maggie; the beer he drank sitting at the kitchen table, an unread copy of the *Manchester Evening News* folded and creased.

— Good day?

— When it's not, you'll know about it.

The same question each night, each night the same reply.

After the gala reception, Gibbs emailed him links to a news report he could watch and a couple of local newspaper stories with pictures. One was of the Bunker, cold and silent, the other was of the museum's curator: a man with a ginger beard; a tubular body sat atop a disarmed missile. Gibbs had met him. Was scathing about what he'd done to the Bunker. He wouldn't say why. You need to see for yourself, old boy, he'd written. Gibbs liked to use old-fashioned English expressions: old boy, jalopy, charabanc, by George, cripes.

Don put down the book and went back to the bedroom.

Maggie had kicked down the covers. He drank from the glass of water on the bedside table and looked down at her. The bed was still warm, the pillows heavy with an unfamiliar detergent smell. He thought about Elvis – young, *King Creole*-era – until he fell asleep.

There was no daybreak, so the lamplight woke him. Maggie had brought him tea, same as she did every morning. She was dressed in an unfamiliar robe with a broken belt loop. He drank the tea though it was scalding hot. She sat on the edge of the bed.

'Are you excited?' she asked.

'I don't know. Nervous, I think.'

'Of course. It's only natural.'

She put her hand to his forehead.

'I almost went. To the Bunker, I mean. The last time I was over.'

'Why would you want to do that?'

'I could always imagine what Jayne looked like,' she said. 'What kind of person she was, but that place . . . ?'

He put his hand on her arm. It weighed there for a time.

'So what stopped you?' he said.

'I wanted you to show me around. Show me now what you couldn't show me then.'

*

When the satnav failed, he directed them from memory. There was a signpost, a nuclear-hazard sign in black and gold, SECRET BUNKER THIS WAY! printed above it. The building itself was a squat, unremarkable structure; grey concrete surrounded by still-fortified metal fences. It could have been mistaken for an electricity exchange or something similar had there not been an aerial atop one of its roofs. There were five cars parked outside, a man leaning against one of them. It was Gibbs. Unmistakable, though he was fat now. Not sweating fat, but big and fleshy. He saluted as the car pulled up.

'Been too long, old boy,' Gibbs said. They shook hands for a long time. 'Shame about Barry.'

'Five years now he's been gone, can you believe it?'

Gibbs finally let go. 'And this must be Maggie's daughter,' he said.

'You don't change a bit,' Maggie smiled.

Don introduced everyone else to Gibbs and Gibbs rubbed his hands together.

'Shall we then?' he said.

The sign at the entrance said EXPERIENCE ALL THE TERROR OF A NUCLEAR WAR – WITHOUT THE RADIATION! Gibbs nudged him and pointed. 'That's just the tip of the ruddy iceberg,' he said.

The lobby was almost as Don remembered it: seating and tables for those on the way to shift or just finishing.

Behind the counter, where Janice used to serve stewed tea, a pair of girls checked their phones. There was merchandise – Russian hats, gasmasks, model warheads, reproduction 'Duck and Cover' instruction booklets – and when the deskphone rang, one of the girls picked it up and said, 'Hello, Secret Bunker?'

Don and Gibbs walked through into an antechamber where a poster explaining the Bunker was pasted: its operational needs and its brief history. It explained nothing, really. The Bunker would house the emergency council in the north-west should the bomb drop. It would keep bureaucracy alive. The others joined them. They read the poster in silence. Gibbs moved through to the next room. Don followed him.

Inside, there was a notice warning younger visitors of a danger facing the Bunker. The Bunker had been infiltrated by Soviet spy mice and it was the children's patriotic duty to find each one of them, especially their most cunning leader, Boris the Rat. James picked up a photocopied sheet printed with the names of ten spy mice and took a pencil from a mug with a mushroom cloud on it. He explained the game to Gracie, how to cross off each mouse when she found it.

'Travesty, isn't it?' Gibbs said. 'The war as bloody theme park.'

'Look, a spy mouse!' Gracie said. Just below the sign,

on top of a missile casing, there was a soft toy mouse with painted, radioactive eyes.

'Maybe the mice we used to see down here were spies,' Don said. 'Wouldn't that be something?' Gibbs laughed and exited the room. Don followed.

On the stairs the old feeling came back. Leaving the dozing world – Jayne, the house in which he lived, the country around him, even Maggie – and heading into the real one. From distraction to knowledge, from inaction to responsibility. The changes in the smell and the light, the changes in ambient noise and sound of voices and machines, they gave him a kind of swagger, a sense of purpose. He knew the truth. He knew what was really going on.

In shifts Gibbs and Don had checked the lines, fixed faults, ensured all the equipment worked. They saw the whole of the Bunker, each of the rooms. Not everyone got to do that. At changeover they'd drink their tea upstairs and go over the job sheets. Not even their wives knew where they were. At the end of the shift Gibbs would say, 'And back to the world of dreams.'

Don passed a photograph, large and grainy, of a mushroom cloud, a 'Duck and Cover' photo strip. Gracie found another spy mouse. It was in the old comms room, peeking out from the cuff of a radiation suit. Don wanted to sit down. The room used to hum with noise:

non-specific, electrical. The chief comms officer had sat at a desk in the centre of the floor space, flanked on his left by Barry and on his right by a younger man whose name Don could not recall. They had been a determined lot; committed, serious. The desks were still there, the phones a mismatch of styles and ages.

'Remember installing them?' Gibbs said pointing to a series of handsets. 'It was a bugger, wasn't it?'

'Three weeks, and only half ever worked properly.'

Gibbs shook his head.

'See the size of them computers? I remember thinking they were tiny,' he said.

Gracie found another spy mouse under one of the telephones and crossed it off her list. Behind her, an outline of the UK glowed on a board, pin-pricks highlighting the eleven post-bomb administrative areas in the event of fall-out. Gibbs went over to it; put his hand on the rope guard.

'She's a lovely kid, your Gracie,' he said.

'Yes, she is,' Don said.

They stood there for a moment, looking at the map. The formations and drills they'd practised, the timings measured and their performance quantified. The Bunker had been closed in '94 and there had been a party. Not quite a party. A few of them and some Scotch and some wine. A speech from Barry. Words recycled from another war, a different victory. Afterwards Gibbs and Don had sat in the comms room until they were asked to leave.

Don walked the remaining rooms in silence. There were mannequins at some of the stations. One behind the desk in the broadcasting suite, another in the infirmary. They made Don jumpy. As though old colleagues had been frozen and wax-covered. He passed through the dormitories to where the council would meet when the time came. All those years and it didn't look in any way familiar. He remembered meeting Maggie. He remembered hearing about her children for the first time. He remembered when one of their weekends was cancelled because James had broken his arm.

Maggie found him standing by the generator. She put her arm around him.

'How did you ever cope?' she said.

He kissed her on the top of her head.

'Come on,' he said. 'We should catch up with the others.'

They met James, Andrea, Gracie and Gibbs at the foot of the stairs, crowded by a door.

'Who's coming in?' said Gibbs.

'Are you serious?' Maggie said reading the warnings written on the door.

Gibbs and Don laughed.

'Well, I'm not going in there,' she said. 'It gives me the creeps, the very idea.'

The rest followed Gracie who, realizing there were no spy mice inside, was heading down the corridor holding the sheet of paper, intent on capturing Boris the Rat. The two friends remained by the door.

'After you,' Gibbs said. Don nodded and pulled the handle.

Inside, the smell was heavy and right; its size, its contents, the small lavatory, a pair of benches, also right. On the wall there was a large red button. They both sat and Don pushed the button. The room filled with static. There was an alarm, one that they both recognized; a female voice they didn't.

'Rose did this part the best,' Gibbs said. Don nodded.

'This is not a test,' the voice said. 'Repeat, this is not a test.'

The bombs were on their way. The voice started a countdown. At the word 'impact', the recording crumpled and there was a low roil, the first inkling of explosion. The lights flickered on and off and the rumble began. Gibbs looked at him, but Don had his eyes closed. The attack went on. The thick doors, the lavatory, the benches all shaking. Then a respite and just a low whistling. Their jobs would start now. After the blast and everything else.

'Tasteful, isn't it?' Gibbs said.

After the bunker had been decommissioned, Don had got a job locally. Jayne was over forty. Too late now. Too late for so many things. He missed Maggie and he missed the Bunker. Jayne lost all patience with him. If you'd have asked him then, Don would have said the Bunker had been taken out just at the right time. It would be better to start again than save the world they lived in now.

Jayne left him for someone else and he spent years in itinerant contracts, jobs here and there. He did not go looking for Maggie. He wanted to, but he had promised. Eventually Maggie found him, tracked him down with surprising ease. He was reluctant. There was nothing to salvage. It would just be the two of them, divorced, eating dinner. Yet more time wasted. But then he let her win. Because he still loved her, he let her win.

The room stopped shaking. The recording finished. The experience was over. Gibbs stood up and opened the door. Don stayed where he was. Gibbs nodded and let the door slam shut.

Don looked at the door and then at the red button. He pressed it again.

'This is not a test,' the voice said. 'Repeat, this is not a test.'

As the low roil started, the door opened. Maggie sat

down on the bench next to him. They let the door slam and the world end around them. They sat side by side until the world stopped ending. The rumbling stopped and there was silence. Then Maggie pushed the button one more time.

WHAT'S GOING ON OUTSIDE?

Karel sat at the card table peeling his third orange. His hands were large and powerful, his fingers nimble. By the time he'd finished, the orange flesh was clean and perfectly round. He admired his handiwork, then split the orange into segments. He ate them quickly, as though one might be stolen at any moment. When done, he sucked the juice from the fingers of his left hand and with his right removed another orange from the plastic sack at his feet.

'For the love of God, Karel,' Eugene said. 'How many oranges can one man eat?'

Karel looked up from his fourth orange, his nail already under the peel. The older man – canted, pocked face, grey-eyed – was stretched out on the right-hand bed, a newspaper just below his eyes.

'Would you like one?' Karel said. 'I have plenty.'

'Speak Russian, Karel!' Eugene said. 'It's almost midnight. It's much too late in the day for English.'

'Would you like one?' Karel said in Russian. 'I have plenty.'

'You know I can't abide oranges,' Eugene said. 'You know I can't stand the way you peel your oranges. So just be quiet, okay? Be quiet and eat your fucking oranges.'

The answer was nine: one man – or at least the man who was Karel – could eat nine oranges in one sitting. The last two are not pleasant: too sweet by that point, too sticky on the fingers no matter how many times you wash them. And their room is the furthest away from both bathroom and kitchen. Those last two oranges are something like an ordeal; but Karel always likes to push things. That's what his father used to say. What Eugene says too.

'Does it not give you a stomach ache?' Eugene asked, setting aside his newspaper and tapping a cigarette against the wall.

'They're on special offer downstairs,' he said. 'A whole bag for a pound. And they're good oranges too.'

Karel held out a segment of orange, Eugene pointed to his lit cigarette.

'They're good for you,' Karel said. 'Vitamins and things.'

'Nothing's good for you,' Eugene said. 'Everything's going to kill you one day. Don't you read the papers? Don't you watch TV?'

'No one's ever died from eating oranges.'

'Perhaps no one's eaten as many as you. Maybe you'll be the first man to die of oranges. The first man to eat his body weight in oranges and then drop dead.'

Karel laughed. His shoulders went down and up like he was working the jackhammer. He stopped and went back to his orange.

'Your father would never have eaten fruit the way you do.'

Karel looked up from peeling. He smiled.

'No, he'd have eaten the peel as well,' Karel said.

'Don't you be disrespectful,' Eugene said.

Eugene shook his head and picked up his newspaper. Karel watched him move from the bed to the window. It was a broken sash, three floors up. They had the best room because Eugene had been there longest and had got to choose both his roommate and where he slept. When Karel had first arrived, he'd shared a bedroom with five other men, sleeping in shifts, the smells and noises like a farmyard. Now there was a wardrobe and a dresser, a card table and two single beds. Eugene opened the sash and hung out, smoking his cigarette. He could smell exhaust fumes, sweet pastry being baked. Most of all he could smell Karel's oranges.

'What's going on outside?' Karel asked.

Their room was above a greengrocer and looked out

onto the main road. The shops were Turkish, Kurdish, Greek; open all hours. There was always something to see, either down at street level or in the flats and bedsits opposite. In the smaller window at one o'clock to them, a man was jigging a small child up and down. He wasn't wearing anything on his top half and was animatedly, though to Eugene mutely, singing as he bounced the child around.

'There are a few lights on. The man with the baby's there.'

'The wife?'

'No. No ladies tonight.'

'There never are any ladies, are there?'

'No. They're all such *teases*, aren't they?' Eugene said.

Karel peeled his fifth orange. He admired his handiwork, then split the orange into segments. He ate them distractedly.

'I'm not sure I can take another night of this,' Eugene said.

'You say that every night,' Karel said. 'Every night the same.'

'Is it any wonder? And stop with the English again. Talk Russian! You sound like a dope in English.'

Karel said nothing in either language. Nothing twice. He ate the sixth orange slowly.

'So out with it,' Eugene said eventually. 'You look like a fish. A big stupid fish.'

'There's nothing to say,' Karel said. 'Nothing important at least.'

Karel started on the seventh orange. The peel did not come away in a perfect roll. The peel looked ragged, like a label picked from a beer bottle.

'How long have we lived together? How long have we known each other? You are my son. My blood is not your blood, but you are my son, as close as is possible. Like Joseph to Jesus. I know, Karel. I know that something is on your mind. Your father looked the same way when things were on his mind.'

Karel put down the half-peeled orange and stood. Triangular torso, bullet-headed, smooth pink skin. The woman he did odd jobs for called him Tank. She liked to watch his forearms as he moved gravel from one part of the garden to another, drinking tea with her friends as he worked. She was a good woman. She reminded Karel of his mother.

'It's nothing, Gen. Nothing really.'

'Say nothing then. Say nothing for the rest of the night. Let's sit ourselves in silence! You can look like a dopey fish all evening.'

There was half of the orange left. It sat on the plate by its torn peel. He looked up at Eugene and then back down at the orange. Were he to say something the conversation would last the night. The thought tired him enough to leave the last of the orange.

Eugene stubbed out his cigarette on the outside wall. Below him, almost touched by the fading ash, were two men arguing outside the greengrocer's. One was carrying a large leather Bible. A bus rattled past. A van with a defective exhaust.

'What's going on outside?' Karel asked. 'What's the noise?'

'Two men are arguing,' Eugene said. 'I don't know the language, but it's an argument.'

'Anything else?'

'There are a few lights on. The man with the baby's still there. His wife now too. They're all singing. She has a top on, but he doesn't.'

'How do they look?' Karel said.

'They look tired,' he said.

*

Karel sat at the card table. By the time he'd finished, the flesh of the tenth orange was almost pithless.

'And you're just going to sit there, are you?' Eugene said. 'Eating your oranges? Eating one after another?'

The tenth one tasted of nothing; the eleventh one same. Karel was not even bothered by the stickiness of his fingers. There had been twenty oranges in the plastic sack and he felt he could eat them all.

'What's wrong with eating oranges?' Karel said.

'It's the way you eat them,' he said. 'Your father would be ashamed at the way you eat them, the way you peel them, with your long nail.'

'Nina likes the way I eat oranges,' Karel said. 'She says it's like art.' He picked up the perfect coil of peel to show Eugene.

'Does she know how many you can eat, though? Does she have any idea of the smell? And speak Russian, for the grace of God!'

'She's normal. She likes the smell of oranges,' Karel said in Russian.

'She says that now, but believe me she'll soon—'

'Can you just be quiet and let me eat my oranges?' Karel said and looked the other way. Half of the twelfth orange remained. It would dry up there, pucker in the summer evening's breeze.

Eugene tapped a cigarette against the wall, went to the window and opened the sash.

'Are you seeing her tonight?'

'We're meeting at ten.'

'You're going out that late? You need to be up in the morning. We have a job.'

'I'll be awake.'

'No good will come of this. Let me tell you that.'

Eugene lit his cigarette and looked out of the window, down onto the street. All the men and women, all the boys and girls. He wondered what Karel's mother would make of it all. What a woman, what Nastia, would make of this house of men. The smells and manners, the grubby nests of sheets. Nastia whose face appeared at the computer screen when he was out. Eugene was always out when Nastia and Karel talked. He did not want to see her, hear her. The way she spoke, the way the words sounded from her mouth. Not like that, anyway.

'What's going on outside?' Karel asked.

'There are a few lights on. The man with the baby's there. Jigging him up and down.'

'He's too rough with that boy,' Karel said. 'Every night too rough.'

'The child's got wind. Even I can see that.'

'He's too rough with him.'

'Since when did you think that?'

'I've always thought that,' he said.

*

Karel took no time or pride in peeling the first orange. He ate a quarter in one, then a half. Then peeled another.

Outside the Turkish restaurant a woman with tightly pulled-back hair was smoking a cigarette. Eugene watched

her take a phone from her handbag and press a button.
Karel's phone rang. He answered it, licking his fingers.
Eugene watched the woman speak. He heard her talk into
Karel's ear. He heard the frustration in Karel's English.
His manic corrections. He heard him say no three times;
say no three ways. Eugene watched the woman end the
call. She looked to the window where he was smoking.
He waved and she walked away, up towards the bus stop.

'Are you not seeing her, then?' Eugene said.

'Not tonight, no,' Karel said in Russian.

'You go and see her, don't worry about me. Don't let
me ruin your fun.'

'You wanted to watch the football together. I told her
that's what I was doing.'

'But—'

'No,' Karel said. 'We watch the football.'

Karel had a laptop and when Eugene was in they
watched American cop shows, Russian soap operas,
British football. It was a nothing match that night, but
they sat on their beds, the laptop propped up on a crate,
and drank bottles of Budweiser. At the end of the game,
Karel's phone rang. He answered with apologies, but
moved on to anger.

'Trouble in paradise?' Eugene said when the call had
ended.

'I'm going to bed,' Karel said. 'A long day tomorrow.'

'Every day is long,' Eugene said.

'She's a beautiful girl, that Nina,' he said. 'But the most beautiful women are from Minsk. I remember the first—'

'I must sleep. Please, Gen, let me sleep now.'

'It's not even eleven.'

'I know, Gen. I know.'

*

It was a Saturday and so there was vodka. Eugene was by the window, smoking the last of his cigarette, a glass in his hand. Outside three women were hailing a taxi, a kid in a baseball cap was talking loudly to another boy, the windows opposite empty save for nets and curtains.

'Were you always in love with my mother?' Karel said.

'Yes,' Eugene said. 'Always. Everyone knew that. Your father used to make jokes. When I was a young man they called me the lapdog. I didn't care.'

There were piles of rind and pith and ribbons of peel on the plate in front of Karel.

'Does she ever talk of me?' Eugene asked.

'She says you're the kindest man she's ever known.'

'Ah!' he said. 'You know what that means.'

Karel took a sip of his vodka and his phone vibrated in his pocket.

'Maybe,' he said, 'in another life you could have been my father.'

Eugene wanted to strike him. To get up from the bed and cuff the boy around the ear. So stupid a reaction; this man, his not-son, was the size of a bear, had arm muscles to make boxers seem girlish. He could never hit him. Would never have hit him.

'I wouldn't have made much of a father,' Eugene said and sat down at the card table. 'You were lucky there. Your mother was lucky too.'

It had changed nothing: his story, his confession. He'd hoped the boy would understand. That men who wander fall in love easily. That Karel's mother was just the first and therefore most pungent of memories. That Eugene knew best. Karel peeled another orange and Eugene went to the window, opened the sash.

'What's going on outside?' Karel asked.

'The man and the woman and the child are there. They—'

Eugene looked over his shoulder and Karel was talking on his phone in a low voice. As he listened to Nina, he mouthed sorry in Russian.

*

Eugene plotted his route again on the small map, though he already knew exactly where he was heading, how long it would take and where to get off the bus. Karel's laptop was useful now he knew how to use it. He'd been on Google Earth and had seen the road on which Karel lived. There were no shops, no bedsits and studios running like a mezzanine above them; just blocks and blocks of flats, trees outside on the pavement, cars double parked in white-lined bays.

Despite the planning, Eugene was a half-hour early. There was a pub around the corner and he drank an expensive bottle of Budweiser while a large crowd watched the rugby. He ordered a vodka and the bar staff, as accented as him but better dressed, served him his drink. The customers were eating roast dinners, drinking wine and beers and Bloody Marys. The pitch of the referee's whistle cut through the loudness of their voices. Some of them looked at him. He downed his drink and headed out the door.

There were forty-seven buzzers outside Karel's block. He pressed number twenty-two and Karel answered as quickly as peeling an orange. He was buzzed through and Eugene took the stairs two at a time. Concrete-grey. A smell of something new, recently fabricated. At the top of the stairs he saw a long corridor with a single door open. Karel appeared, wide smile on wide mouth, waving with his goalkeeper's hands.

'Gen!' he called out down the corridor. 'So good to see you!'

'And you, Karel, my boy,' Eugene said. 'But speak

Russian, boy, it's Sunday. Don't you know to speak Russian on a Sunday?'

'Come on in, Gen,' he said in Russian after they embraced. 'Come see my new place.'

The flat was ferociously tidy, three rooms – kitchen/living room, bedroom, bathroom – with laminate flooring and the cheapest kind of furniture. The small table was set for three. Nina was stirring a large pot on the stove. She looked like she had been stirring the pot for a hundred years.

'I brought something for you,' Eugene said and took out some beers from his shoulder bag.

'Thanks,' Nina said. 'Good to see you, Gen,' She kissed him on the cheeks.

'You're looking well,' he said tapping her stomach. 'It must agree with you.'

She nodded and Karel put his arms around her. She pushed him away and went back to stirring the pot.

'We have a balcony too,' Karel said and opened the fridge, poured beer for them both. 'Let's go outside, yes?'

They opened the door onto the smallest balcony Eugene had ever seen. It was just about big enough for them to stand side by side. There was an ashtray set on a very small wooden card table.

'So how are you?' Karel asked.

'Fine. You?'

'Fine,' he said. 'Excited.'

'You have a lot to be excited about.'

Eugene smoked a cigarette and they both drank their beer and both agreed how good it was to see each other at last. Then Nina called Karel inside to help with serving lunch.

Nina was a fine cook and Eugene had three helpings of stew.

'You can come any time, Gen,' she said.

'Thank you, Nina,' he said. 'I would be honoured.'

After they had cleared the plates, the two men went outside again. The wind had got up and there were teeth in it. They agreed the food was good, that Nina was a fine cook.

'I have something for you,' Eugene said as they went back inside. Out of his shoulder bag he took a plastic sack and handed it to Karel.

'Here,' he said. 'I thought you must be missing them.'

'Thanks, Gen,' he said. 'Look, Nina, Gen has brought us oranges!'

'Oranges?'

'Yes, look, from the shop I used to live above. Best oranges I ever tasted.'

'They were nice, yes,' she said and shrugged everyone back to the table.

Karel sat at the table peeling an orange. By the time

he'd finished, the flesh of the orange was clean, pithless and perfectly round. He passed the plate with the orange to Nina. She split open the orange and quickly ate it. He peeled another, split it, and quickly ate. Eugene watched the two of them, the juice on their chins, the way they licked the juice from their fingers. He watched them smile and with his right hand, Eugene took an orange from the plastic sack. He dug in his thumbnail and began to peel.

LIVE FROM THE PALLADIUM

The man bends down and asks: 'What do you want to be when you grow up?' After the pause, after the raising of the eyes, I deliver the line Mother has taught me. 'When I grow up, Mr Hughes, I want to be a proctologist.' Mother laughs. Mother shakes her head. Mother puts on her finest Jewish accent: 'My son, the proctologist!'

The best jokes exist in the present tense: man walks into a bar; your momma; knock-knock. This is something Mother says when we talk about comedy. I am nine years old the first time I tell the proctologist joke. It is a success and Mr Hughes takes us home in his big car. The following night I am allowed to sit up with Mother and watch the videotape of my father. He performs the brown-suit routine and we laugh like it's the first time. The best jokes, she reminds me, exist in the present tense. 'You can depend on a joke,' she says. 'A joke is always happening.'

There are faded colour photographs of Mother in her youth, drink and cigarette in hand, laughing with men who were once well-known. Mother has high, arching eyebrows, a bowed mouth, long painted nails; she is dressed impeccably, stylishly. You cannot ignore her glamour.

She knew the hotel bars where the pier entertainers drank and would approach them if she'd enjoyed their act. She slept with some; provided others with material. This she tells me.

'One of mine,' she tells me once, twice; again, again, 'was on the *Royal Variety Show*. Old Roy came out on stage all fat and sweaty in that dinner jacket that never fitted, and he says' – Mother adopts a broad northern accent – '"My wife said we should experiment more in the bedroom. After two weeks, I'd discovered a cure for cancer and now she's left me. Some women are never satisfied."'

The following Saturday, Mr Hughes picks Mother up in his big car. Mother has asked our neighbour Serena Jenkins to babysit. I am obviously, shyly in love with Serena Jenkins. I will never smell hairspray without thinking of her; will never hear Whitney Houston without seeing her shift from left to right in her tight denims.

The sofa is old and surprising with springs; it is made for two. I sit next to Serena and put my feet up on the coffee table in a way I am not allowed. The flat is tidy for once. There are vacuum-cleaner skids in the nap of the thin brown carpet, polish smears on the windowsill, a new air-freshener beside the television.

'Do you know what I want to be when I grow up?' I ask Serena after I've poured her a glass of Coke.

'What's that, little man?' she says.

'When I grow up, Serena, I want to be a proctologist.'

She sips her Coke and puts it down on the coffee table.

'That's nice,' she says and looks down at her homework. In her textbook there is a picture of Gandhi; in her exercise book her rounded, bubbly handwriting. I assume she hasn't heard what I said.

'Yes,' I say. 'That's what I'm going to be: a proctologist.'

She closes the textbook on her index finger and turns towards me. She hasn't laughed twice. Everyone always laughs.

'What's a proctologist?' she says.

*

Mr Hughes invites us to live with him. He has a big house with a garden, four bedrooms, a garage. Also a big television and two bathrooms. I am thirteen and it's the best thing that could have ever happened to us. Even Mother says that. But we make heavy work of leaving the flat. The move takes over two months, always an excuse found to stay another day, another week. There is no pressure from Mr Hughes, he reminds us of that, but he seems confused as to why we spend so many nights a week back at the flat, huddled by the gas heater watching videos.

'I'm going to miss this place like cystitis,' Mother says. 'Like thrush.'

'Like a boil on my cock,' I say.

'Like a bitten tit,' she says.

A month, two months of this, and we are living with Mr Hughes.

'How do you like your new bedroom?' Mother asks as I come down the stairs, my skin still pink from the power shower.

'It's so much better than the bedroom I had last week,' I say. 'There's a double bed for a start.'

'A double bed? Which side do you sleep on?'

'Whichever one's dry,' I say.

Mr Hughes watches us laugh, and eventually he joins in; though his thick face and reedy moustache suggest tension, perplexity even. He is roasting a chicken and the house is clean and warm and homely; as though he has been waiting much longer than three years for us to arrive. He has prepared roast potatoes and homemade stuffing balls; for afters a gooseberry crumble with real custard. He pours us glasses of champagne as a welcome to our new home.

'Mr Hughes?' I say. 'Do we get champagne before every meal?'

'Only special dinners,' he says, smiling. 'And call me John.'

'Well, Mr Hughes, every dinner's special to me,' I say. 'You never know where the next meal's coming from with her' – I thumb towards Mother – 'I've lived my life in fear of being sold into the white slave trade.'

'It can still be arranged,' Mother says and we both laugh, and a little later Mr Hughes joins in, again with the tension, again the perplexity. That look becomes the poor man's constant, niggling expression. I never call him John. After a few months he stops even mentioning it.

When I turn sixteen, Mr Hughes tries to talk to me (the man has always tried; he is very trying). He feels this is the kind of conversation a man should have with a boy looking down the barrel of adult life. I know this because I heard him say so to Mother. I am in my bedroom; a Woody Allen stand-up record is playing on the turntable he bought for me.

'Can you turn that off for a moment?' he says.

'It's the moose routine,' I say.

He clicks off the record and sits on my bed.

'We need to talk, Clive,' he says.

'What about?' I say.

'Well,' he says. 'I've always said that I'm not here to

replace your father, but there are some things that are best said man-to-man, so I thought—'

'Oh, Mr Hughes, I know all about sex,' I say. I have been preparing this for a few days and I'm watching Mr Hughes for a reaction. His eyes are wide: this is good.

'Yes, Mr Hughes. I know all about sex. You really don't need to worry. I know all about it. I know all about foreplay, fingering, heavy petting, hand-jobs, tit-wanks, cock-sucking, cunny-licking, sixty-nines, straight sex, missionary sex, rough sex, anal sex, gay sex, lesbian sex, roleplaying, threesomes, foursomes, bondage, frotting, felching, rimming, fisting, golden showers and pegging.'

He shakes his head and stands up.

'Well, it's hard not to,' I say. 'My room's right next to yours.'

He slams the door on the way out.

'Ooh, shut that door,' Mother shouts from downstairs.

Not long after our little talk, Mr Hughes comes home with a red setter. He walks the dog whenever he can, no matter what time of day or night. I call it Mr Hughes, though Mr Hughes calls it Ivanhoe. Mother and I both think this is a funny name for a dog. She always calls it Steve.

If we are in the hallway when Mr Hughes is ready to take Ivanhoe out, Mother points at the dog.

'I say, that dog's got no nose,' she says.

'How does it smell?' I reply.

Mr Hughes mouths the punchline and slams shut the door.

Mother and I say, 'Ooh, shut that door.'

The best jokes, she says, get better with repetition.

Mr Hughes checks into a hotel on the night of the first episode of the third series of *Blackadder*. Mother only cries after the credits roll. For the first time in months we watch Dad performing the brown-suit routine. We rewind the tape, watch it back, rewind the tape, watch it back. Again, again, again.

'I love the way he winks just then,' Mum says replaying a section midway through his five minutes. 'It's just perfect.'

'It's great, yes.'

'When he forgot his lines, when he was too drunk, he used to do that wink. Then he'd say. "I only have to wink at a bird and she gets pregnant."'

I feed the line. 'Is that what happened with me?'

'No,' she says. 'The rubber split, but the effect was pretty much the same.'

We laugh and later run through some *Round the Horne* and *Goon Show*. 'You have deaded me,' she says as we go up the stairs. She is wobbling drunk and holds on to the sleeve of my shirt. 'You have deaded me,' she says again, but does not laugh.

*

We call the new flat 'the corridor' for its narrowness – we both love the Four Yorkshiremen sketch – and I keep it tidy, despite Mother's best efforts. I do homework at the small table and she watches videos. Men come and go, quoting lines from *'Allo 'Allo!*. They do not. This is my joke and Mother doesn't find it funny.

'The only wasteland I know,' she says after I have explained it, 'is between the ears of the men who write *'Allo 'Allo!*.'

Men do come and go, though, in the night, in the morning. Mother still looks sharp on her legs, her chest high and supported; her heart-shaped face underneath the elegant yet slightly old-fashioned do. They are always gone when I wake. They are nothing like my father; they are nothing like Mr Hughes. Mother and I joke in the same way, still feed each other lines, but we laugh less than before. Sometimes she sounds like she's just playing along. Even when I say, 'To cut a long story short,' and she says, 'Too late,' it doesn't sound like her heart is quite in it.

*

Mother perches on the edge of the bed. I am sitting at the small desk, writing. For a moment I think she's going to start on like Mr Hughes.

'It's all right, Mum,' I say. 'I know all about the birds and the buggery.'

She laughs and something lifts slightly in her brow, then falls.

'Trouble at mill?' I say.

She starts to cry. Her face make-up darts like military manoeuvres on old maps.

'It's my fault,' she says. 'It's all my fault.'

'What?' I say. 'What's your fault now?'

'This . . .' she says. 'This . . . hiding yourself away. Always at home, always . . . I don't know, making dinner, tidying up. It's never normal. I blame myself, I should—'

'The only thing I blame you for is the Suez Canal Crisis, you know that.'

I put down my pen and smile but she doesn't even pout. She says nothing. It's like a pause for timing, but she has nothing more to say.

'Honestly, Mum, I'm fine.'

'No you're not,' she says. 'It's not right your being here the whole time. What about friends?'

'When I was growing up we were so poor, we couldn't afford friends.'

'I give up,' she says.

She slams the door behind her. Neither of us says anything.

A week later she comes back from a night out. I am watching the video of my father. The brown-suit routine. She sits down next to me, damp from rain and fog.

'I've fixed it,' she says. 'You're booked.'

I press pause. Dad is standing there, about to imitate an Irish glue sniffer, a roll of Sellotape soon to emerge from inside his brown jacket pocket.

'What?' I say. 'What have you booked?'

'You. Cyclone Club. Monday week. First act up. Five minutes.' She sniffs and wanders to where she keeps the whisky.

'You're not serious.'

'Do I ever joke about comedy?' she says and pours herself a drink. Her face says *Gotcha*. Since the slammed door, this has been her threat of choice: get out of the house, or I'm putting you on the stage.

'I'm not doing it,' I say. 'I can't do it.'

'Don't be such a child, of course you can. We'll write it together.'

'You do it.'

'Me?' she says. 'Oh, give over. I've told you this before: there are no funny comediennes. There are funny *women*, but no funny comediennes. Name one that's any good.'

I've heard this before; I know how it plays out. I follow the lines, hoping it will swing her off topic.

'Joan Rivers.'

'Joan Rivers? An unconvincing drag act with a voice like a synagogue on fire.'

'Roseanne Barr.'

'Roseanne? Like a sack of lesbian potatoes shouting in a mini-mart.'

'French and Saunders.'

'Double acts don't count. The fact is that alone on stage, women look desperate and whorish,' she says. 'And I hate to look desperate.'

She gets up and looks at her reflection in the mirror. Tests the bounce of her hair.

'Think about it,' she says. 'Think about it at least.'

'Okay,' I say as she ruffles my hair. 'But I'm not promising anything.'

'It'll do you good, love,' she says. 'Promise.'

She pauses by the door.

'And you'll get sex,' she says. 'Lots and lots of sex.'

*

For inspiration we go through Dad's old material, the odd jokes he wrote down on menus and cigarette packets, snippets of things he overheard in pubs. Dad was a listener, but not much of an archivist. He was a present-tense comedian. Died young and with him most of his gags.

We spend the weekend working on the routine, then weeknights working on delivery. She borrows a video-camera from Pam at work – *God knows what she records on this normally* – and sets it up in the lounge. I start the routine. Nervously and without conviction.

'Fuck off,' Mother shouts. 'You're shit.'

I do not react well to her heckles, not well at all. I stutter as I try to move on to the next line, but she's shouting over me, calling me a poof; a fucking nancy boy.

'Mum,' I say. 'Please.'

'You need to learn,' she says. 'There's no point in playing nice. Remember that comedy is not only commu-nion between performer and audience, but also between every constituent part *of* that audience: friends in groups, couples, people on their own. Remember that.'

The argument starts there; the tape still spooling. The video shows my eighteen-year-old self shouting back at her, her shouting louder, telling me that if I want to succeed, I've got to toughen up. She makes no jokes in fifteen minutes of argument, not even an attempt at one. Had Mr Hughes seen that, he might not have ended it. After twenty-three minutes I disappear from shot. You can hear the slam of my bedroom door.

'Ooh, shut that door,' Mother shouts.

*

The Cyclone is a club on the northern edges of the city. Backstage, I meet the three other comedians: an Englishman, an Irishman and a Scotsman. No joke. The Scotsman has slept with Mother. This I know for certain: it's him who's got me the gig. The comedians do not speak to me; they just sit on old armchairs drinking bottled beer, talking loudly to each other.

'You said you'd never come back here. Not after what happened,' the Scotsman says.

'Apparently they're only really brutal to you the first time around,' the Englishman says.

'Yes,' the Irishman says. 'The first time I came here I was crying piss by the end of the night.'

The compere is out on stage doing his routine. It is stitched together from better performers' work. I hear my name being called and the Scotsman pushes me in the back. I come stumbling out onto the stage, into the light. No one laughs. The lights are not as bright as I had expected. I can see the audience, no more than forty strong, and Mother at the bar. I pause for timing purposes. The best jokes exist in the present tense.

'I've heard you lot are a tough crowd,' I begin, 'but before you say anything, please remember that I was born with ginger hair and I'm an orphan. Until I was twelve, everyone called me Annie.'

Beat.

'It's been a hard-knock life, I can tell you.'

Beat.

'Not many fans of musical theatre in tonight, I see.'

Beat.

'Like I said, I'm an orphan. My father died young. I still remember the last thing he ever said to me. Remember it like it was yesterday: "Son, please, please, please stop throwing knives at me." '

Beat.

'My mother died very soon afterwards. I don't remember her last words. It was hard to make them out over all the screaming.'

Beat.

'There's nothing funny about that, lad,' a fat man near the front shouts. He is sitting next to a fat woman.

'My, my,' I say. 'I used to be as fat as you, sir, but now you're on benefits, your wife can't afford to give me a biscuit after I fuck her.'

There is a collective intake of breath and a few sly chuckles. I smile, sweetly, like a child. It's mainly the women who laugh.

'My dad actually did die young. That's true. No joke. He was killed in the Falklands.'

Beat.

'It always was a rough pub.'

Beat.

'I'll tell you how rough it was. This bloke walked into the Falklands once and says to the barman, "What sort of wine do you have?" and the barman says, "Bottle or glass?" "Oh, glass, please," the bloke says and the barman smashes a pint pot in his face.'

Beat.

'Like I said, rough place.'

Beat.

'After my father died, my mother, she remarried. On the morning of the wedding my new dad took me to one side and said: "Clive," he said. That's my name, he was clever that way. "Clive," he said. "I'm going to treat you like my own flesh and blood. I'm going to treat you like you're my real son." And he was true to his word.'

Beat.

'From that moment on he ignored me during the week and beat me senseless every Saturday night.'

It goes on. Five minutes. The audience is confused and annoyed by my deadpan delivery, by the one-liners, by the uneasy subject matter. It's a relief when I can call time on the whole sorry mess.

'I have been Clive Porter,' I say. 'And you have been my worst nightmare.'

I walk quickly backstage as the compere bullies the audience into patchy applause. The Englishman, Irishman and Scotsman are still on the armchairs drinking beer. The Englishman opens a bottle and passes it to me.

'You don't have a day job, do you, son?' he says.

'When you get one, don't quit it,' the Irishman says.

When we're back home and she's poured us both whiskies, Mother tells me what I have done well – the right level of menace in my put-downs, my timing on some of the weaker jokes – and what I have done badly – stage presence, clarity, poise, switch from set-up to punchline, pitch of voice, facial expressions, audience interaction and volume.

'Your dad would have been proud of you, though,' she says. 'Yes, he'd have seen talent there. Real potential. And anyway, it's a laugh, isn't it? What could be better than making someone laugh?'

'Making ten people laugh?'

She punches me on the arm.

'Honestly, your dad would be proud.'

Two nights later she goes out with the Scotsman to say thank you. I have another gig arranged soon afterwards.

*

The best jokes and routines improve with repetition; they appreciate. The only people who tire of them are the comics themselves. My favourite routine of all time is recorded the same year I make my stage debut. Palin is stage right, smoking a cigarette, dressed as a shopkeeper; Cleese enters stage left holding a birdcage. Audience applauds. They laugh before a word has been said. Cleese says he wishes to make a complaint. Wild laughter, wild applause. There are thousands watching in the theatre; millions who watch it later. The audience knows every word. Each of them has their favourite synonym in Cleese's litany of death; each one is ready to join in. The sketch follows the usual pattern, with Palin asking what the problem is and Cleese explaining that he wishes to complain about the parrot he has just bought. Palin asks what's wrong with it; Cleese explains that it's dead. Wild, wild, laughter. Palin pauses and takes an exaggerated look at the deceased bird. Palin glances up at Cleese. The audience giggles nervously. Palin puffs on his cigarette and says, 'So it is. Here's your money back and some holiday vouchers.' The audience laughs, but are cheated. Cleese and Palin, twenty years on and still having to do that fucking parrot sketch. So sick of it, they have to kill it dead. It's easy to understand; I feel the same necessity even during my third show.

What's funny at home, funny with Mother, is not

funny outside the flat. I want to ad-lib, freshen up the routine, but I have nothing. I just stand there, microphone in hand, running through the same lines, the same actions. Mother makes notes. This is the new thing: not laughing, just making notes. The audience laughs sometimes, laughs because they are predisposed to. They like the swearing; they like that they need do nothing more than laugh.

Unasked, the Scotsman puts in calls for me, recommends me. Unasked, Mother accepts on my behalf. Unasked, I am booked for six consecutive nights in various places across the south-east.

'Isn't that great news?' Mother says as she holds me, tight enough to let me know I cannot decline.

'Yes,' I say. 'It's great news.'

That evening, I stay up and watch my father again on the video, his five minutes of fame on *Live from the Palladium*. He must have done that routine a hundred, a thousand times up and down the country. I was probably conceived a few hours after he'd delivered it at some club in Great Yarmouth. The cassette tapes of his act, which he used for bookings, is the same routine, but just his voice, not his skinny body in the trademark brown suit. I take the tape with me on tour; listen to it in guest-house rooms as the Scotsman and my mother have hushed but audible sex next door.

The first night is fine, the second the hecklers are vicious, violent. The men are drunk and hateful; they do not wish to laugh with but at. I watch my mother and she looks oddly calm, then strangely confused.

'Well done,' she says afterwards.

'That was horrible,' I say.

'You were brilliant,' she says and looks for all the world like she believes it. She does believe it. The next night she is laughing, no longer making notes. She can see it. There is no future in it, just the constant fucking present.

*

The last date is the biggest one on the itinerary. The Irishman joins us on the bill. He doesn't recognize me and I have no interest in talking. I have a couple of drinks, and from backstage see my mother by the bar, an old guy chatting her up. For a moment, just for a split second, he could be Mr Hughes. But he is not Mr Hughes, just a man in a blazer, laughing loudly. It turns out that he is the compere; a filthy, innuendo-soaked old queen popular with the local students.

'Apparently he's a real cult,' says the Irishman to the group of us, pointing over to him as he helps himself to a glass of wine. 'Or at least that's what I read in the *Guardian*.'

Everyone laughs but me; it is a joke I do not quite understand. Mother is still at the bar, now checking her eye make-up in a compact mirror. She does not belong here, surrounded by students in their DM boots and cardigans and limp, long hair. She looks out of time as much as out of place. I watch her until I'm given the nod.

The applause is warm, just as it is at the Palladium. I salute left, and I salute right. I stand in the centre of the stage and it all comes so easily; it's the last gig and it's all so easy.

I stand there and when I can take it no longer, when there is just a sense of audience unrest, I do the wink.

'Hello, ladies and gents, my name's Davey Cruz,' I say.

'I only have to wink at a bird and she gets pregnant,' I say and look down to the front row. 'Are you looking forward to raising me bairns, sir?'

I do the low reassuring laugh.

'I'm only kidding!' I say. 'I can't help it, me. I'm just a kidder, you know. This one time though this bloke, true story this, ladies and gentlemen, this bloke tried to attack me live on stage, as I was actually performing. Which is why I always wear a brown suit on stage. Just in case I have another little accident.'

The intonation, the accent, the stance, is purely my father. I'm not wearing a brown suit, but I do the brown-suit routine anyway. The room is nervous, the laughter sparse.

'You're shit,' someone shouts.

'No, sir,' I say, 'it's just the brown suit. You need to get your eyes tested.'

It's an ad-lib from the cassette version of the routine. It comes at around the right time and I try the little tip of finger to nose gesture he was good at. It works perfectly. I do the whole routine, line for line, word for word, ending exactly the way my father had.

'My name's Davey Cruz. Don't go changing – I won't recognize you.'

I turn away and see myself as a child, backstage, in the wings, standing beside my mother. Mum is young and applauding my father, her face set with joy. I turn back to the audience one last time, just as my father does on the video. Mum is standing now, applauding. Members of the audience are turning to look at her, the crazy woman clapping alone. She ignores them and continues to applaud. I can hear her even when I'm finally backstage.

She still talks about it. When she remembers. When she's more lucid. But even then it's hard to know whether she's talking about me or my father. Perhaps it's both. At the hospital, she tries her best, but jokes won't be wrangled the way they once were.

'Are you a doctor?' she asks when I arrive.

'I'm your son,' I say.

'But are you a doctor?' she asks again.

'I'm a proctologist,' I say.

'That's right,' she says. 'My son, the proctologist.'

Acknowledgements

A grant from The Society of Authors provided time and space to write some of this collection. Its generosity is gratefully appreciated.

This book would not have seen the light of day without the guidance, help and patience of Andrew Kidd. Thank you, and good luck.

Kate Harvey for her editorial wisdom and continued support. Lucy Luck for stepping in as though she's always been there.

Stuart Wilson for the cover, Nicholas Blake for the copy edit, Camilla Elworthy and everyone at Picador.

Nick Royle at Salt, Philip Davis at *The Reader*, Rachael Allen at Granta for publishing early versions of these stories. Ra Page and Steven Amos for commissioning 'Swarm', which benefited from the consultation of Pepe Falahat; Rowan Routh for excellent early editorial input.

Susan Ruszala, Kristina Radke, Lindsey Rudnickas, Tarah Theoret and everyone at NetGalley/Firebrand.

Suzanne Azzopardi, GJ Bower, Niven Govinden, Lee Rourke, Nikesh Shukla, Chimene Suleyman.

Acknowledgements

Jenny Offill, Eimear McBride, Teju Cole for their kind words.

The Chequers, E17, for excellent editing facilities.

William Atkins for his quiet wisdom. Nicci Cloke for being brilliant at whatever she does. Barbara Baker and Eugene Sorokin; Simon Baker and Hilda Breakspear. Gareth Evers and Matt Baker.

Oliver Shepherd for always being there; Daniel Fordham and Jude Rogers for inspiration both musical and written.

My mother and father, Joyce and John Evers, for setting the benchmark.

Lisa Baker and Caleb Evers. To the ends of the earth.

In memory:

Stephen Callender (1951–2014).

Molly Evers (1923–2014). YNWA.